DEAR GOD,
HELP!!!
LOVE,
EARL

THE GEEK chronicles

3

DEAR GOD, HELP!!! LOVE, EARL

Barbara park

A YEARLING BOOK

Published by Yearling, an imprint of Random House Children's Books
a division of Random House, Inc., New York

Yearling and the jumping horse design are registered trademarks of
Random House, Inc.

Visit us on the Web! www.randomhouse.com/kids

Educators and librarians, for a variety of teaching tools, visit us at
www.randomhouse.com/teachers

ISBN-13: 978-0-679-85395-4
ISBN-10: 0-679-85395-2

Reprinted by arrangement with Alfred A. Knopf
Books for Young Readers

Printed in the United States of America

First Bullseye Books Edition April 1994

First Yearling Edition July 2006

10 9 8 7 6

To every kid who's ever
been bullied,
beaten up, or otherwise
pushed around—
Hang in there.
Your day will come.

—B.P.

CONTENTS

DEAR GOD,
HELP!!!
LOVE,
EARL

1 DEATH WEARS SHORTS

Death is in my P.E. class.

I know him personally. He has brown hair and freckles. And he wears baggy shorts.

A lot of people think that Death wears a black hooded robe and has long, white, bony fingers. But that's only in the movies. In real life, Death has a tan, and he bites his nails right down to the nubs.

He's got a name, too. Death's name is Eddie McFee.

I met him the first week of school this year. He didn't introduce himself, exactly. He was sitting in the first row of the baseball bleachers, and when I walked past, he tripped me.

I don't mean I just stumbled over his foot, either. 'Cause when Eddie McFee trips you, he knocks your feet out from under you and you go crashing to the ground. Hard.

A whole lot of kids started laughing. But not Eddie. He just leaned back in the bleachers, folded his arms, and watched me real serious-like. You know, as if I was some kind of lab rat or something.

My face turned beet red. It felt hot, too. Embarrassingly hot.

"Ha ha. Very funny," I managed.

But Eddie still didn't smile. "Oh, come on, Tubs," he said. "You're just trying to be nice. It wasn't *that* funny."

My stomach knotted up when he called me that name. *That's not who I am,* I wanted to say. *My name is Earl Wilber. And from now on, you use it.*

But saying something like that to Eddie McFee would have been totally gutsy. And I'm not the gutsy type. I mean, I have a few guts, I suppose. But mostly I just use them for digestion.

Anyhow, after you've spent a whole lifetime listening to kids make fun of the way you look, you sort of learn to accept it after a while. You learn to keep your mouth shut, too. 'Cause if you don't, it only makes things worse.

Like one time in first grade, this kid named

John Paul Potter called me Miss Piggy during recess. Which was totally insulting, especially since Miss Piggy is a girl and all.

So I walked over to John Paul. And I said, "Sticks and stones will break my bones, but names will never hurt me. HA!"

I did the big HA! right in his face.

That's when the chase began. John Paul Potter and about a hundred of his closest friends started chasing me all over the playground. It finally ended when Gloria Biddles lassoed my foot with her jump rope and I fell face-first into the grass.

I'm allergic to grass.

I started to wheeze so bad I had to use my squeezy nose drops and my mouth inhaler.

The next thing I knew, John Paul and Gloria were skipping in a circle around me, singing, "The cheese stands alone…the cheese stands alone…hi-ho the derry-o, the cheese stands alone."

Only, instead of singing the word "cheese," they were singing the word "wheeze."

"The wheeze stands alone," they sang.

I still remember closing my eyes and wishing that the ground would open up and swallow me down to the middle of the earth. That way I would never have to see those mean kids again. Or hear their teasing voices.

As usual, though, the ground didn't cooperate. But I can tell you one thing for sure. When I finally went back to my room that day, I promised myself I would never recite that lame "sticks and stones" thing again. Which is why I didn't even consider sticking up for myself against Eddie McFee.

Still, I couldn't help wondering why he automatically hated me so much. I mean, I know I'm a little on the heavy side. And fine, I'm wheezy and I have a cowlick. But there's cool stuff about me, too. Like I'm a good friend, I think. And I have a pretty big heart and all.

Like last spring I stayed up two nights in a row feeding a baby bird that had fallen out of its nest. It ended up dying. But that was my mother's fault. She made me go to school on Monday morning. And when I got home, my cat, Chuck, was prancing around the house with the bird in his mouth, like it was some sick little prize he'd won at a cat carnival.

I cried over that bird. I buried him in a box

lined with flowers. I even made this little cross out of some twigs and junk I found on the ground.

Not that Eddie McFee would care about that side of me. To him I'm just somebody to pick on.

In fact, after that first day in P.E., it was almost like I became his weekly entertainment. You should have seen the way his eyes would dance around when he would get me alone in class. He'd either trip me or bang my head into the lockers. Other times he'd give me one of those hard knuckle-punches in the arm.

I didn't tell anybody about it, though. Not even my best friend, Maxie Zuckerman. Let's face it, there are some things just too humiliating to say out loud.

Unfortunately, Maxie found out anyway. One day he accidentally walked into the bathroom while Eddie was flushing my head down the toilet.

As soon as Eddie looked up, Maxie backpedaled out of the bathroom so fast you wouldn't believe.

"Oops! Sorry! Didn't mean to barge in on you, Ed," he blabbered as he left. "Just, you know…go back to what you were doing."

Maxie only weighs about eighty pounds, so I didn't really blame him for that. Trying to come to my rescue would have been a suicide mission. Anyhow, as soon as Eddie had left the bathroom, Maxie rushed right back in to help me.

"Earl! My God!" he said, upset. "You've got to tell somebody what he's doing to you. I mean it. You've *got* to."

I narrowed my eyes at him. "No, I don't. I don't *got* to do anything, Max," I told him. "Just forget it, okay? Just pretend it never happened."

Maxie looked at me like I was nuts. "Pretend it never happened? Are you serious? I can't just pre—"

"Yes, you can!" I snapped. "I'm not telling anybody *anything*. Get it? Not Coach Rah. Not my mother. Not anybody. Do you know what Eddie McFee would do to me if I ratted on him? He'd pound me into bonemeal and serve me to his dog for Thanksgiving dinner. Believe me, Max. He's already explained it to me down to the goriest little detail. So just forget what you saw, okay? This is none of your business."

After that, I slicked back my hair, which was

still wet from the toilet, and walked out of the bathroom.

Maxie didn't bring it up again. And—right or wrong—I never squealed on Eddie McFee.

I did try hiding from him one time, though. You kind of owe it to yourself to try hiding from Death at least once, I think.

I got to the gym early that day and squeezed behind one of the tumbling mats hanging on the wall. Unfortunately, Eddie spotted me before I was totally hidden. He lifted up the mat and gave me a grin that sent chills up my spine.

"Boo," he said quietly.

My upper lip quivered as I tried to smile. "Um, well, yes, boo to you, too, Ed," I said.

He laughed. "You weren't trying to hide from me, were you, Jumbo?" he said.

Then he reached in, grabbed my arm, and yanked me out as hard as he could. After that, he marched me into the boys' locker room and shoved me against the cinder-block wall. My head hit the wall pretty hard, too. I didn't cry, though. I never cried in front of Eddie. At least I'm proud of that much.

"Why can't you just quit it?" I asked him. "Why can't you just leave me alone, Eddie? What did I ever do to make you hate me so much?"

For a split second, Eddie looked confused. "*Hate* you? I don't hate you, Earl," he said. Then he pulled me up right next to his face. "You and me are just havin' fun."

A minute later, I was in a headlock, and the two of us were running all over the floor. "See? Isn't this fun, Tubs?" he said.

He jerked me harder.

Suddenly, four quarters came flying out of my shirt pocket. They hit the floor and rolled for a while.

Eddie stopped to see how many there were. And I'm telling you, it was like a miracle almost. Because at that exact moment, I got an idea that was so great I couldn't believe it.

"Wait!" I yelled out. "Hold it, Ed! Watch this!"

Then, as fast as I could, I picked up the money and shoved it into his hands.

"Here!" I said. Then I felt in my pocket for the two dollar bills. "Money! For *you!* Wow! What a great brainstorm I'm having here! Look at this! I brought three dollars to buy a book at the book fair today. But instead, I'm giving it to you! Get it, Ed? I'm paying you to stop hurting me!"

For a second, Eddie just stared at the money in his hands. Then all of a sudden, his whole face lit up.

"Whoa! Earl! You just might have something here, dude," he said. "This *is* a good idea."

He stuffed the money into his pocket and patted it in there. "Yeah. I definitely like this. It's kinda like we're two businessmen doing a deal, right? For three bucks a week, I don't break your neck."

Quickly, I shook my head. "No, Ed. No way. I can't pay three dollars every single week. I don't have that much money. I swear. I can only bring you one."

He thought it over. "Two," he said finally. Then before I could say no, he grabbed my hand and made me shake on it.

So from that day on, that became our little arrangement. Every Wednesday morning before P.E. began, I would give Eddie McFee two bucks, and he didn't lay a hand on me.

I could stroll around the gym wherever I pleased. Sit wherever I wanted to. Say whatever I felt like saying. And Eddie didn't raise an eyebrow.

At first it just seemed so perfect, I couldn't believe it.

But, as it turned out, there was one little glitch with our arrangement that I hadn't really thought of. Because the thing about money is that—unless you come from a rich family—sooner or later it runs out.

And I don't come from a very rich family.

My mother is an assistant manager at Milo's Market. So we're not exactly raking in the bucks.

She's been divorced from my father since I was three. Dad sends child-support money every month, but he's not rich, either. After their divorce, he moved back to England, which is where he was born. But I don't know what he does, exactly.

I think I'm supposed to miss him, but I don't. He's an okay guy and all, but my mother and I have a lot more in common than me and my father. Like we don't call our oatmeal "porridge." And we never use the word "bloody" unless something is actually bleeding.

Also, my father calls his umbrella a "bumbershoot." How can you feel close to a man like that?

Anyway, since Mom doesn't make that much money, the main cash I get comes on birthdays and holidays. I keep it in a sock in the back of my underwear drawer. That's what I was paying Eddie with.

I knew it wouldn't last forever. But one night when I was getting my money for P.E., I turned my money sock inside out and counted how much I had left.

"One…two…three…four…"

I gasped. No! This couldn't be true!

I shook the sock all around in the air, but nothing more came out.

"Four?" I said. "Oh, man! There has to be more than four dollars left! There were at least eighteen bucks in there when I started!"

My stomach knotted tight as a drum.

Two more payments. That's all I had left. Two more payments, and I would be Eddie McFee's punching bag again.

I crawled into bed and stared up at my ceiling.

In desperation, I started to pray.

"God?" I began. "Excuse me, okay? But it's Earl Wilber down here. Remember me? I'm the one who asked you to vaporize that kid in my P.E. class a few weeks ago.

"Okay…well, apparently you didn't feel right about that. And I respect that, okay? But see, now my money sock is almost flat, so I really need you to take me seriously this time.

"From now on, I need to be sick on P.E. mornings, okay? Not forever, I don't mean. Only until the holidays. Just till my Christmas money comes in. I mean it, God. All I need is a little rash or a fever on these mornings. Or maybe one of those twenty-four-hour stomach flu things.

"But whatever sickness you choose, remember…it *has* to be something that my mother can either see or measure with a thermometer. Like don't just give me a headache, or she'll hand me a couple of aspirin and I'll be at school so fast it'll make your head spin.

"Okay. Well, I guess that's about it, God. I'll let you get back to whatever you were doing. Meanwhile, I'll be right here in my bed waiting for my infection.

"This is Earl Wilber, thanking you in advance.

"Over and out."

2 NOSY ROSIE AND OTHER PAINS

The next morning I was fine. Seriously. I'd never felt better in my life. No temperature. No rash. No nothing.

I looked up at my ceiling and frowned.

"Okay, I realize you're busy, God. But even Federal Express can deliver by ten A.M."

"Earl!" hollered my mother. "Who are you talking to in there? It's late! Are you dressed yet?"

My mother has the biggest ears in the universe. Also, her morning voice sounds like fingernails scratching across a chalkboard.

I pulled a sweatshirt over my head. "I'm almost ready," I hollered back.

I probably would have been more upset about having to go to school, but during the night, I had come up with a backup plan to get out of P.E. Even when you're counting on God to infect you, it's always good to have a backup plan, I think.

Mine was the nurse's office. If I didn't wake up sick, I would go to school, fake an ankle injury, and spend the day with Nurse Klonski. When it comes to faking illness and injuries, Nurse Klonski isn't a pushover, exactly. But still, it was worth a try.

Before I left my bedroom, I stuffed two dollars in my jacket pocket. If my backup plan failed, I definitely didn't want to have to face Eddie McFee empty-handed. Just the thought of it made my stomach so queasy I had a swig of Pepto-Bismol with my breakfast. After that, I ate two Rolaids and left for Maxie's house.

Since Maxie lives right across from school, my friend Rosie Swanson and I meet him on his porch and we walk the rest of the way together. The three of us only met at the beginning of the school year. But we're already best friends. That's because we're all kind of oddballs, I think.

Take Maxie, for instance. Even though he's real scrawny, he's got the biggest brain in the entire school. Like he's never gotten anything below an A+ in his whole life. And his hobby is reading the dictionary. I'm serious. He finds weird words that no one's ever heard of, then he teases you with them. Like he'll call you a scrum, for instance. Which has something to do with rugby, I think. But when Maxie says it, it sounds totally insulting.

As for Rosie, she's the snoopy, tattletale type. Her grandfather used to be a cop, so she's always trying to force Maxie and me to cross at cross-walks and stuff like that.

We still like her, though. Maxie says she's *resolute,* whatever that means.

Anyway, as soon as I turned the corner for Maxie's house that morning, I looked down and saw one of my dollars creeping out of my jacket pocket.

"Oh, geez," I said right out loud. The last thing I needed was for Rosie to start asking a bunch of questions about why I was bringing money to school. Paying Eddie McFee not to hurt me was humiliating enough without my friends finding out about it.

Just as Rosie came running up beside me, I

grabbed the dollar out of my pocket and hid it in my fist.

"Come on, Earl. Let's go!" she said, rushing past me. "We're late. If we don't run, we're all going to get late slips this morning. Hustle!"

I hate it when people tell me to hustle. In my opinion, a kid should be the boss of his own speed.

I kept right on walking. "Hustle yourself," I said.

As usual, Rosie wouldn't take no for an answer. She grabbed my hand and started to pull me.

Unfortunately, it was the hand with the dollar bill.

"Hey! What's in your fist, Earl? Is that money sticking out of there? What are you bringing money to school for? Is the PTA selling those brownies you love again?"

I didn't answer.

Rosie kept at it. "Come on, Earl. Tell me. Why are you bringing money to school?"

"Nosy," I said. *"Nosy Rosie."*

"Earl!"

"It's for none of your beeswax, that's what it's for," I told her.

By now, we were almost to Maxie's house. He was sitting on the porch step waiting for us.

"Max! Hey, Max!" Rosie shouted. "Earl's hiding money in his fist, and he won't tell me what it's for!"

Maxie raised one eyebrow like he was Sherlock Holmes or somebody.

"Oh?" he replied.

"*Oh* yourself," I said. "What's wrong with you guys, anyway? I brought a couple of lousy dollars to school. Big dumb deal. It's just for an emergency, okay? Haven't your mothers ever told you to carry money in case of an emergency?"

Rosie shrugged. "Mine hasn't," she said. "She taught me CPR and the Heimlich maneuver. But she never said anything about bringing money to school."

"Mine either," said Max. "In case of an emergency, I'm supposed to call my uncle Murray, the personal injury lawyer."

He reached into his book bag and pulled out two business cards. He handed them to Rosie and me. The cards said:

IF YOU'RE HURT AND LIFE'S NO FUN,
CALL ME AND WE'LL SUE SOMEONE.
Murray Zuckerman
Personal Injury Attorney
555-3546

"He's an excellent lawyer," Maxie told us. "My uncle Murray can make you think you've been injured, even if you haven't."

I rolled my eyes and started across the street. That's when the school bell began to ring.

Rosie took off like a rocket. The thought of getting a late slip totally freaks her out. Maxie was hurrying, too.

"See you in P.E., Earl!" he called.

Even though the two of us are in different rooms, all the fifth-grade boys have P.E. together on Wednesday mornings.

I crossed my fingers. Not if I can help it, I thought.

A few minutes later, I was standing in the hallway right outside Nurse Klonski's office. I could see her sitting at her desk. She was rubbing her temples. Nurse Klonski is one of those school officials who always seem to have a headache.

I made a pained face and limped into her office.

"Ouch!" I said. "Ow! Ouch!"

Nurse Klonski looked at me a second. Then she lowered her head to her desk and covered it up with her arms.

"No. Please, Mr. Wilber. Not you. Not today," she said.

I'm not exactly one of Nurse Klonski's favorite people. I'm the only kid I know who's ever gotten a comment from the nurse on his report card. The first marking period she wrote:

EARL MAKES TOO MANY UNNECESSARY VISITS TO MY OFFICE.
NURSE K.

I made my voice sound as weak as I could.

"I'm sorry to bother you, Nurse Klonski," I said. "But I fell on my ankle coming up the school steps this morning. And I think it might be broken."

Quickly, she stood up. "Oh, my gosh, Earl!

Why didn't you say so? I had no idea this was serious," she said.

Nurse Klonski ran around the desk and started taking off my shoe.

"Ow! Ow! Ow! That kills!" I yelled.

She pulled her hand away. "But I barely even touched you."

"I know, I know. It just hurts, that's all," I whined.

She tried one more time.

"Ow! Stop! Please!" I hollered even louder than before.

By now, she seemed seriously worried. "It looks like you're going to need to have this X-rayed, Earl," she said. "Do you have school insurance?"

I shrugged. "I don't know. I can't remember. Is an X ray expensive?"

I looked around the office. "If an X ray is expensive, maybe we could just prop my foot up on some pillows for a while and see if the swelling goes down on its own. I don't mind lying here if it'll save my mother an X ray bill, Mrs. Klonski. Really, I don't."

I sat down a second. Then suddenly, I frowned.

"Shoot. Of all the crummy luck. I just remembered. I have P.E. this morning."

I sighed. "Darn it all. I *love* P.E., too. But I guess I'll just have to miss it today. Right, Nurse K.? I mean even if my ankle is better by ten o'clock, I still don't think I should put any weight on it. Do you?"

At first, Nurse Klonski just looked at me. Then all at once, she seemed to relax a little bit.

"I think you're right, Earl," she said. "And I agree that we should hold off on the X rays for a while, too. Wait here a minute, okay? I'll go round up a few pillows to help elevate your foot."

She went to her office door and started into the hall.

That's when I heard her shriek.

"OH, MY STARS IN HEAVEN!"

Then, quick as anything, she ran back into the office, slammed the door, and leaned against it with all her weight.

"Good gosh! You will not *believe* what's coming down the hall!" she said.

I flew to the door. "What? What? Tell me! What is it? What's out there?"

I started jumping up and down, trying to see

21

through the little window at the top. But I couldn't jump high enough.

Still leaning against the door, Nurse Klonski crossed her arms and looked down at my foot.

"My, my, my. Look at that. Our broken ankle seems to be feeling better," she said.

I stopped jumping right away. But it was too late.

I was already busted.

I didn't speak for a really long time. Instead, I just stood there with my cheeks turning hot from embarrassment.

Finally, I swiveled my ankle all around. "Gee. What do you know? It's a miracle," I said softly.

"Hallelujah," said Nurse Klonski. Then she opened the door and stepped out of my way.

I backed into the hall. "All rightie. Well, uh...have a nice day," I said stupidly.

She said, "Ta-ta," and shut the door.

A few seconds later, I heard a tapping sound on the little window. When I looked up, her fingers were waving at me.

I don't think I'll be going back there again. Not for a while, anyway.

* * *

Mrs. Mota dismissed us for P.E. at ten o'clock. I still remember how sick I felt walking to the gym that morning.

As usual, Eddie McFee was waiting for me in the boys' bathroom. That's where I always gave him the money.

I took one look at him and blessed myself. I'm not Catholic, but I'm pretty sure anybody can bless themselves. Like the Catholics don't own it or anything.

Eddie gave me one of his normal friendly greetings. "You got the money, Jumbo?" he asked.

I handed over my two dollars. "Yeah, sure, Eddie. Here," I said. "But before you go, there's something I need to talk to you about."

The muscles in Eddie's face tightened. "Like what kind of something?" he asked.

I took a deep breath. Then, trying to keep my voice calm, I started explaining all about how broke I was. And how maybe if we could lower the payments, my money would last longer.

"This is only a temporary problem, you understand, Ed," I said. "I'll be getting more money at Christmas. But until then, if we just lower the payments, at least you'll still be getting a little something every week, right? And something is better than nothing, don't you think?"

Eddie didn't think at all. Instead, he grabbed me by the shirt and pushed me against the wall. Then he put his foot on my stomach and pressed so hard I thought I would split in two.

"This is a joke, *right*, Tubs?" he asked.

As I doubled over, I managed to nod.

Eddie sneered. "Good," he said. "Because if I don't keep gettin' my money, that would upset me. And if I get upset, I might do something to you that doesn't feel so good, Earl. You know, something like this."

Before I knew it, Eddie McFee had grabbed ahold of my ears and was practically lifting me off the ground. I'm not exaggerating, either. It felt like he was ripping my ears right off my head.

My eyes filled with tears. I wasn't crying, exactly. But I was getting close.

Eddie saw. "Oooh nooo. What's da twouble?" he said. "Is da widdle baby stawting to cwy?" he teased.

He let go of my ears and shoved me back into the wall. Then he pointed his finger in my face.

"Don't ever joke around about not giving me my money again, Earl," he warned. "I need this money, okay? I *count* on it."

He stood there glaring a little while longer. Then finally, he left.

I washed my face and followed.

3 TORTURE

I was still trying to brush Eddie's dirty footprint off the front of my shirt when Maxie sat down next to me on the bleachers.

He stared at the mark. "Who danced on your stomach?" he asked.

I turned away from him. "Nobody, okay? Just never mind."

Suddenly, Coach Rah came hurrying into the gym and gave a loud blast on his whistle. "Kickball today, gentlemen!" he shouted. "Today's captains are Paulie Little and Leon Lucas. Paulie? Leon? Get down here and choose up sides, men!"

Paulie and Leon hurried to the middle of the floor and started scanning the stands to see who they wanted to pick. But even though I was sitting up straight and tall, their eyes passed over me like I was the invisible man.

I always get picked last. Always. Ever since kindergarten, it's been the same thing. I sit in the bleachers while the captains start choosing up sides.

Then one by one, the rows begin to empty until there's only six or seven of us left.

Then there's four.

And then there's just me and one other kid.

That's when I cross my fingers and pray that this time—just this once—I won't get picked last.

Then the other kid gets chosen.

And there I am…

Sitting all alone.

And it's like I'm wearing a giant sign that says EARL IS A LOSER.

And it feels like torture, I'm telling you. Absolute, total torture.

And okay, I know there are other tortures that are worse. Like I wouldn't want to be lowered into a pit full of snakes. And one time my mother made me watch that whole *Nutcracker* thing on PBS.

But what makes being picked last especially hard to take is that Eddie McFee is always chosen first. *Always.*

A lot of people don't know this, but Death is

27

an excellent athlete. He's real coordinated and all. Like you should see the cool way he strolls onto the floor after he gets picked. Even with rubber soles on, he practically glides.

This time Paulie Little won the toss.

"Eddie McFee," he said right away.

"Gee. What a surprise," I mumbled to Max.

I slumped down in the bleachers. "It's not my fault that I'm not a good athlete, you know. I mean, geez, my father's from England. They don't even *have* sports over there."

For some reason, I felt myself getting annoyed. "Did you know my father's name is Cecil? Cecil Halliwell Wilber III. Yeah, boy. That really sounds like an athlete's name, doesn't it?"

My voice got louder. "Guess what his favorite sport is, Max? This'll kill you."

Maxie gave me the "shh" sign. But I was suddenly so angry, I couldn't seem to control my volume.

"No, really. Come on. Guess," I insisted.

Maxie reached over and tried to cover my mouth. But he wasn't in time.

"DARTS!" I hollered out. "The man plays darts!

He's even got his own special little dart box that he carries around with him! Can you believe that?"

I made my voice sound British. "He says it's JOLLY GOOD FUN!"

Coach Rah glared up at me from the floor. "Hey, Prince Charles. You wanna put a sock in it, son?" he shouted.

Everyone busted out laughing.

God! Why did it always have to be like this? At least half my life has been spent in total humiliation.

I closed my eyes and plugged my ears to block out the noise. I knew it wouldn't work, though. No matter how hard you press on your ears, you can never keep the laughter out.

By the time I finally opened my eyes again, there were six kids left on the bleachers.

Then four.

Then there was just Maxie and me.

It was Paulie Little's turn to choose.

I crossed my fingers. Come on, God. Just this once, okay? Just this one time don't let me be the last one picked.

"Zuckerman," called Paulie.

Leon Lucas looked irritated. "Great," he said. "I get Prince Charles."

It takes guts to walk down to the gym floor after being laughed at. Most people never think about that. But I'm telling you it takes real courage.

It definitely doesn't put you in a good mood, though. As Maxie and I walked out to the kickball field, he was blabbing away like crazy, while I wasn't saying a word.

It was weird, too. Because even though I could hear his voice, I had absolutely no idea what he was talking about.

Finally, he gave me a shove. "So what about it?" he said. "Can I borrow the money or not?"

I stared at him blankly. "What money?"

Maxie hit me in the arm. "You haven't heard a single word I've said, have you? The two bucks you brought to school…I forgot my lunch and I need to borrow it."

I stopped dead in my tracks. *No.* Please. This could *not* be happening. Hadn't I been through enough for one morning? Did I actually have to make up an on-the-spot lie about where my money had gone?

I felt myself start to panic. "No," I blurted. "You can't have it, Max. You can't borrow it."

Maxie gave me the meanest look ever. "Well, thank you, Mr. Generous," he said. "Thank you, Mr. Good Friend. Mr. Emergency Money. Mr. My Best Pal. It's not like I wasn't going to pay you back, you know."

He started to walk off.

"No. Wait, Max. You don't understand," I said. "The money's gone already. I don't even have it anymore."

Maxie turned around and raised that stupid Sherlock Holmes eyebrow of his. "So where did it go?"

I swallowed hard. *Come on, Earl! Think! Think! Where did the money go? Make up something. Quick!*

"Well, uh, let's see. The truth is…I gave it to someone," I said.

Maxie's eyebrow refused to go back down. "Like to who, exactly? Who did you give it to?" he asked.

I began to stutter. "To who? You mean, you want to know the actual person I gave it to? Because, well, um…let's see. I gave it to…"

31

Think, think, think! Who do people give their money to?

"The Salvation Army," I spouted.

Maxie looked at me like I was a lunatic. "*The Salvation Army?* Are you kidding me? You mean the guys with the bells and the little red pots at Christmas?"

By now, I was totally flustered. "Yes. Right. They're the ones. A Salvation Army guy came to my room this morning for Show and Tell. And when he clanged his little bell, I automatically put my two dollars in his pot. I couldn't even help myself, Max. I'm conditioned to do that. I swear. My mother makes me give them my allowance at Christmas."

It was a ridiculous lie. No one in their right mind would have believed it. Especially not someone as smart as Maxie.

I watched as his eyes drifted back to Eddie's footprint on my shirt.

I tried to cover it up again. But I knew I was too late.

Maxie Zuckerman's brilliant brain was already putting two and two together.

4 UNCLE MURRAY

Maxie didn't waste a bit of time telling Rosie about my lie in P.E. At lunch he kept ducking behind my back and whispering to her. Then later, while the three of us were walking home from school, they started giving each other these stupid signals with their eyebrows.

I caught Rosie right in the act.

"Stop that," I said. "You two have been whispering about me all day, and I'm sick of it."

Rosie turned to Maxie and nodded. "You're right. He *is* being a kaka."

"Kaka" is one of Maxie's stupid dictionary words. I think it's some kind of bird. But it sounds like something a lot worse.

"I am *not* being a kaka," I said. "You're being a kaka. You're both kakas, in fact. You're the kaka twins. So there. Ha."

Maxie tried to settle me down. "Come on, Earl," he said. "We weren't telling secrets about you. We're just trying to figure out what the heck's going on with you, that's all."

I felt myself tense. "What do you mean? Why do you think that something's going on? There's nothing going on. I swear."

"Oh, really?" said Maxie. "Then why did you make up that stupid lie about what you did with the money you brought to school this morning?"

"It wasn't a lie," I lied. "I told you the truth. I gave my money to a Salva—"

Rosie put her hand over my mouth. "Save your breath, Earl. A Salvation Army guy wasn't in your room today. I checked it out with the principal's office."

I started to sweat. I couldn't believe they were after me like this. Why didn't they just mind their own business?

"Oh, yeah? Well, guess what, Miss Giant Snoop Head?" I said. "The office didn't even know about it, probably. I bet the Salvation Army guy was an old friend of my teacher's or something. In fact, I think that's what Mrs. Mota even told us. She said that she used to be in the Salvation Army, too. And she and this guy went to basic training together."

Rosie rolled her eyes. "The Salvation Army doesn't send people to basic training, Earl. It's not that kind of army."

Maxie put his arm around my shoulder. "You're a terrible liar, Earl. We know there's something going on that you don't want to tell us."

He looked again at the faded footprint still on my shirt. Then he softened his voice a little.

"It's got something to do with Eddie McFee, doesn't it?" he asked.

My blood went cold when I heard that name. I should have known Maxie would figure it out. The kid buys brain teaser books for a hobby.

There was no sense pretending anymore.

I walked over to his porch step and sat down. Then I hung my head so low they couldn't see my face and I whispered the shameful secret I'd been keeping inside.

"He makes me pay him, Max," I said quietly. "I pay Eddie McFee two dollars a week not to beat me up."

Maxie winced. "I *knew* it. I was sure it was

something like that," he said. "I've had a feeling there was something going on for a long time now. But it wasn't until P.E. this morning—when you had that footprint on your shirt, and no money—that I finally put it all together."

He gave me a sympathetic pat. Then he reached into the front pocket of his backpack and began to dig around. A couple of minutes later, he pulled out another one of his uncle Murray's business cards and pressed it into my hand.

"Sue the creep," he said.

I looked at him strangely. Maybe I hadn't heard him right.

"What? What did you say?"

"I said, *sue him,* Earl. Sue the creep," he repeated. "What Eddie's been doing is illegal, okay? It's called *extortion.* You've heard of that before, right? Extortion is when somebody forces you to pay him money by threatening to beat you up or kill you or something. And it's against the law. And I bet my uncle Murray could sue the pants off Eddie's family and really teach them a lesson."

All of a sudden, he began to grin at the

thought of it. "God, what a great country this is," he said.

My mouth dropped open in amazement. "Have you lost your *mind?*" I asked. "Don't you understand how humiliating this is for me? I never even wanted you and Rosie to find out. And now you expect me to blab the whole story to your uncle Murray?"

Maxie frowned. "But—"

"But nothing, Maxie. But forget it!" I said. "I told you before, I'm not telling anybody anything! If anyone finds this out, I'll be the joke of the whole school. Even more than I already am."

I looked around to make sure no one was coming. Then I cupped my hands around my mouth like a megaphone.

"ATTENTION, WORLD! CAN YOU FOLKS IN OUTER MONGOLIA HEAR ME? I JUST WANTED TO ANNOUNCE TO THE UNIVERSE THAT I, EARL WILBER, AM A BIG FAT WIMP! AND I CAN'T STICK UP FOR MYSELF! SO I'VE BEEN PAYING EDDIE McFEE TWO BUCKS A WEEK NOT TO FLUSH MY HEAD DOWN THE TOILET! FILM AT ELEVEN."

I looked at him disgustedly. "Yeah, Max, that's just what I want to do, all right. I want to shout my secret to the world."

After that, I stood up and started walking for home as fast as I could.

"Great, Earl. Just great!" Maxie called after me. "Run away just like you always do. This is so *typical!* You're such a complete wimple!"

I came to a screeching halt. Oh! So now we were into namecalling, were we! Well, two could play that game.

Furiously, I spun around.

"So *sue* me, why don't you? Huh? That's your answer to everything, isn't it, *Mr. Big Fat Lawyer Pants?*" I hollered back.

For a second, Maxie looked like he had been slapped. Then he narrowed his eyes and slowly began walking toward me. He didn't stop until he was right in my face.

"Excuse me," he said dryly. "But did you just call me Mr. Big Fat Lawyer Pants?"

I looked down at him and smirked. "Yes," I said. "That's *exactly* what I called you. I called you Mr. Big Fat Lawyer Pa—"

But halfway through "pants" I started to crack up. I just couldn't help it.

Then Rosie cracked up, too. And pretty soon even Maxie couldn't hold it in. We couldn't stop, either. We laughed until our sides ached.

After that, everything got a little easier.

"Okay. So maybe my Uncle Murray idea was stupid," Maxie admitted finally. "But that still doesn't mean there's not a way out of this problem. Maybe we should all just go home and think about it for a while. Then on Saturday, we can meet at the clubhouse and talk over some solutions. How does that sound?"

I hesitated. How did it sound? It sounded *terrible*. That's how it sounded. The last thing I wanted to do was sit around on a Saturday morning discussing my private, personal, humiliating business.

Then all of a sudden, I remembered! I had an *excuse* for Saturday. A real honest-to-goodness excuse that I didn't even have to make up.

"Uh oh. Sorry, but I can't make it on Saturday," I said a little too happily. "My mother and I have to go to a funeral."

Rosie shivered. "Eww. A funeral," she said. "Who died?"

"I'm not exactly sure," I said. "There's some old lady who comes into Milo's Market every week. And yesterday she told my mother that her best friend died. So Mom offered to drive her to the funeral."

I shrugged. "Hey, who knows? Maybe if I make Eddie McFee any madder, next week it'll be *my* funeral. That'd be one way out of this problem, right?"

Rosie hit me in the arm. "Don't even joke about a thing like that, Earl," she said. "I mean it."

Suddenly, Maxie's mouth dropped wide open. Then his face turned weird. I mean *really* weird. Like at first, he just sort of squinted a little and tapped on his chin. But pretty soon his eyes were totally glazed over like his mind was a million miles away.

After that, he began talking to himself in this hushed, whispery voice. And he kept repeating the word "funeral" over and over again. It was spookier than anything.

Finally, he started rubbing his hands together.

Slowly at first. Then faster and faster, until he clapped real loud.

"Yes!" he said, punching his fists in the air. "I've *got* it, Earl! I've got an idea that will get Eddie McFee out of your life forever! I mean, I don't have all the details worked out yet. But if I put my mind to it, I know I can put it together in no time!"

The next thing I knew, he sped up the porch steps, laughing like one of those crazy scientists. Then he disappeared inside the house without even saying good-bye.

Rosie and I stared at the door.

It wasn't the first time Maxie had ever weirded us out.

And I was sure it wouldn't be the last.

5 TO BATTLE

Maxie worked on his idea almost the whole night. He said he didn't get to bed until three A.M. I believed him, too. Walking to school that morning, he looked all pooped and droopy. And he was still wearing the same wrinkly clothes he'd worn the day before.

But even though he looked totally worn out, he still called an emergency meeting after school. "Three-fifteen. My garage," he announced, yawning. "Be there."

Maxie's garage is where our clubhouse is located. Except it's not really a clubhouse. It's actually an old, beat-up '55 Chevy that belongs to his father. Still, if you lock the doors and roll up the windows, it's a pretty private place to meet.

When we all got there that afternoon, Rosie and I climbed right into the back seat. Maxie always gets the front to himself. It's not fair, but Maxie says when you own the clubhouse, you don't have to be fair.

As soon as the doors were locked, he pulled three reports out of his briefcase and held them up for Rosie and me to see. They were all printed out and stapled together.

"Okay, guys, here it is," he said, handing Rosie and me each a copy. "This is what I was working on all night. *The Plan.*"

I looked at the printed title:

Maxie's Amazing Plan to Get Rid of Eddie McFee
BY MAXWELL ZUCKERMAN
(IQ 160+)

Right away my stomach started to churn. The Plan weighed a ton. I mean, geez, I didn't want to have an epic adventure trying to get Eddie out of my life or anything. All I really needed was a few extra dollars to last me until Christmas.

I tried to hand it back to him. But Maxie had already started to read. "Act one, scene one," he began. "Earl's note."

43

Earl's note? What note? I thought.

Out of curiosity, I opened The Plan and turned to the first page. Then, before I knew it, I was following right along as Maxie read.

The Plan was written exactly like a play—with acts and scenes and stuff like that. Even the actual conversations we would be having with Eddie were already written down for us.

I know I've said it a million times, but Maxie has an amazing brain. If Maxie Zuckerman's brain ever goes on display at the Smithsonian Institute, it probably wouldn't even fit into one of those big mayonnaise jars.

By the time he was finished reading, Rosie's mouth was hanging wide open. "Whoa," she said. "This plan is *unbelievable,* Max."

Maxie puffed out his chest. "Yes, I know," he said proudly.

He turned to me. "So what do you think of it, Earl? It's great, don't you think? I've taken care of every single detail, haven't I? I know we can pull this off, Earl. I'm positive."

I began to fidget. Yeah, sure. I mean, The Plan was unbelievable and all. But it was a lot of other stuff, too. Like risky and dangerous…and *extremely* hazardous to my health.

Maxie leaned over the back seat. "Well? Say something, Earl. You like it, don't you?"

I looked at him and shrugged.

Maxie's eyes opened wide. "*Whatttt?* Are you *kidding* me? You don't *like* it? After all the work I put into this thing, how could you not like it? This plan is *brilliant,* Earl! It's remarkable! It's…it's…"

"Suicide," I said.

Maxie nodded. "Yeah, okay, fine. I admit that some of it will take a few guts on your part. But it's not like you're going to have to do any of this alone, Earl. Rosie and I will be right behind you every step of the way."

"Oh, good," I said. "That'll be the perfect spot for the two of you to pick up my body parts after Eddie gets through tearing me limb from limb."

Maxie looked annoyed at me. "Quit exaggerating the danger," he said. "There's no time during The Plan when Eddie will have the chance to seriously hurt—"

I interrupted. "Have either of you guys ever seen a watermelon bust?" I asked. "That's what my head's going to look like when Eddie finally rams it into the bathroom wall."

Maxie was getting more and more frustrated. "That's *not* going to happen, Earl. I'm telling you this plan will work. Once we get started, we're going to sail right through this thing as easy as pie."

"Sailing makes me vomit," I said.

By now, Maxie was totally out of patience. "Listen, you. This plan isn't just about Earl Wilber, you know. Just because you're the one with the problem right now doesn't mean that the rest of us don't have problems, too. I get pushed around every single day by kids like Eddie McFee. And so does Rosie. And so do a hundred other kids who go to this school."

He narrowed his eyes. "Eddie McFee is *pewage,* Earl. All bullies are *pewage.* And now we have the perfect opportunity to get back at one of them."

He raised his voice. "How can you not understand how important this is? This is *war.* It's us against Eddie McFee. And we can win it. You and Rosie and I can teach Eddie McFee a lesson that he'll never forget."

Rosie nodded her head in agreement. "I think he's right, Earl. I think we can do this."

She patted my shoulder. "Come on. What do you say? Let's crush that egg-sucking roach!"

After that, she and Maxie started whooping it up and high-fiving and junk.

I sat there and watched them.

War is always funnest for those who don't actually have to do the fighting.

Finally, I got out of the car and began walking to the door.

Maxie got out, too. "Wait! Where are you going? What are you doing? We can count on you, right, Earl? I mean, you *are* going to go through with this, aren't you?"

For a second, I just stood there staring back at him.

Then weakly, I gave him a sick salute.

That's what soldiers do right before they go on a dangerous mission. They turn and salute the brains of the outfit.

Then they go into battle.

And no one ever hears from them again.

6 EXTORTION MAN

I took the long way home. There's a shortcut through Maxie's back alley. But back alleys make me nervous. And besides, I needed some extra time to think about The Plan.

I needed a lot of time, in fact. I mean, how could I even be considering such a stupid thing? If everything didn't go exactly right, I could end up *dead*.

And what about Maxie and Rosie? What kind of friends would encourage an overweight kid with no self-confidence to risk his life against the toughest bully in the fifth grade?

I cringed at that description of myself.

An overweight kid with no self-confidence. God, how I hated thinking of myself that way.

Still, as bad as it was, at least it was better than being a rotten jerk like Eddie McFee. So what if I wasn't a fighter? What was so terrible about being peace-loving?

"It's not fair," I said right out loud. "A kid shouldn't have to fight for his right not to fight. It's not even logical."

Without even realizing it, I had stopped walking. Then—even though I was still a block from home—I sat down on the curb and I started to think about stuff. Stuff about the way I looked, I mean. And about the way I was, and the way I wanted to be.

And don't ask me why, because I swear this has never happened before in my life. But instead of getting completely depressed, my mind kept going back to the idea that, even with all my faults, I'd still rather be like me than be a jerk like Eddie McFee.

Finally, with nothing really accomplished, I stood up, brushed off, and began walking again.

For some reason I felt better, though. I can't explain why. I just did.

I don't know where courage comes from, exactly. I mean, I know you don't get stronger from just sitting on the curb thinking about yourself. The only thing I really know for sure is that when I walked in my house that day, I had to go through with The Plan.

I called Maxie after dinner. The first step of The Plan was scheduled to begin the very next morning. I was going to have to write a note to Eddie McFee and order him to meet me after school. But thinking about it made me so sick inside, I needed Maxie to keep walking me through it.

We went over it a hundred times, I bet. But even after the two of us finally hung up, there was still more work for me to do.

First, there was a picture to draw.

And then there was that note to write. The note that would set The Plan in action.

It wasn't going to be a pleasant note, either. It was going to be a nasty note. A *very* nasty note.

"The nastier the better," Maxie had said. "It's got to make him angry, Earl. Just like the picture you're going to draw. They both need to make Eddie furious."

So eventually I drew the picture. And I wrote the nasty note. But the whole time I was doing it, my hand was shaking like crazy. Because writing a nasty note to a kid like Eddie McFee is like writing an invitation to your own murder.

Which—now that I think about it—was *exactly* what I was doing.

The next morning, I was a wreck.

As soon as I got to Maxie's house, I told him that I'd changed my mind. "I can't go through with this, Max," I said. "I thought I could. But I can't."

Maxie paid no attention to me. Instead, he grabbed the notebook out of my hands and started searching through my papers.

"The picture, Earl. Where's the picture you drew?" he asked.

Rosie walked up and said hello.

I ignored Maxie and talked to her instead. "I'm not going through with it," I said. "On the way over here, I thought of a new plan. A better plan. I'm going to run away and live in a foreign land."

Rosie patted my hand like I was somebody's nincompoop great-grandfather. "Sure you are, Earl. Sure you are."

Just then Maxie found the picture I had

drawn. His whole face lit up. "Hey! This is good, Earl. *Really* good! It's perfect, in fact!"

Excitedly, he began searching for the note I had written.

I continued talking to Rosie. "It's going to be a peaceful, happy land. A land where people have to be nice to each other or the army chases you over the border."

Finally, Maxie spotted the note sticking out of my jacket pocket.

"Whew! Good," he said. "For a second there, I thought you didn't write it."

He pulled it out of the envelope and read out loud:

> Dear Edward,
> If it's not too much trouble—and if you haven't made other plans for after school—I was wondering if you could please meet me behind the big tree in the corner of the playground at three o'clock.
> If not, don't worry about it.
> Love (the brotherly kind),

Earl
PS: Kindly come alone.
PPS: Peace be with you.

Maxie glared at me. "Does this sound mean to you, Earl?" he asked. "Huh? Does this sound like the kind of note that will make Eddie mad? I told you a hundred times...if Eddie's not angry, The Plan won't work."

He ripped a new piece of paper from the notebook and scribbled down some words. This time when he read, even Rosie looked grim.

Ed,
After school, dude. Behind the big tree in the corner of the playground. Just you and me.
And come alone, chicken. Or ELSE!
Earl

He folded up the new note and shoved it in my pocket.

I turned back to Rosie. "I'm going to miss you when I'm in my new foreign land. You've been annoying at times, but I'm still going to miss you."

Frustrated, Maxie ran his fingers through his hair. "Come on, Earl, get a grip, okay? We're going to do this, and that's that. Now let's go."

After that, he turned and started walking to school. Rosie did, too. And you could tell by the way they did it that they thought I would automatically follow.

I didn't, though. I mean, part of me really wanted to follow. But knowing what I was going to have to do when I got to school was scaring me to death.

So I just stood there.

Frozen, almost.

Then all of a sudden, it occurred to me. Maybe this was one of those "moment-of-truth" things that happen to a person sometimes. You know, one of those critical times in your life when you have to make a snap decision about what kind of stuff you're really made of. Like whether you're going to follow through with something you believe in. Or whether you're going to turn around and run the other way.

Time was running out.

I closed my eyes and took a deep breath.

Okay. Fine. Just this once, I'll try to follow through, I thought. But it's a one-time-only deal. And I *definitely* don't have to be a good sport about it.

I hollered at Maxie. "OH, ALL RIGHT. I'M COMING! I'M GOING TO DO IT. BUT YOU BETTER HOPE THIS WORKS, BUDDY BOY. BECAUSE IF IT DOESN'T, I'M GOING TO HUNT YOU DOWN AND SQUASH YOU LIKE A GRAPE!"

I heard that line on TV one time, and I've always wanted to use it. It felt good, too. I swear.

After that, I took the note out of my pocket and crossed right in the middle of the street. *Not* at the crosswalk.

Before I knew it, I was standing at the front door of the school waiting for Eddie McFee.

Maxie and Rosie arrived a couple of minutes later.

"Okay. Are you happy now, Einstein?" I said to Maxie. "See me? I'm waiting for Killer McFee with my nasty note, okay? Now you'll get to be

55

the big wizard behind The Plan, and I'll get to be the dead rotting body behind the big tree after school."

I knew I was a little out of control, but growling at Maxie seemed to give me the courage I needed to keep standing there.

Just then the bell rang.

Rosie gave me a hug. "You can *do* this, Earl. I know you can," she said.

Maxie gave me a thumbs-up. "You've got nothing to worry about. I promise."

A second later they were gone, and I was standing there all alone. Waiting for Eddie.

My heart was pounding so hard I thought it would come right through my chest.

Desperately, I closed my eyes and shot up a quick prayer. *Dear God, HELP!!! Love, Earl.*

When I opened them again, Eddie was coming around the corner of the building.

I sprang at him. "Hey, McFee!" I yelled. Then I shoved my note into his hand. "This is for you!"

After that, I took off for my classroom as fast as I could.

* * *

I still don't know where I got the nerve to meet Eddie at the tree that afternoon. I guess way deep down, I knew that Maxie and Rosie wouldn't let anything really bad happen to me. But still, I was the scaredest I'd ever been in my entire life.

Halfway to the tree, I stopped and tried to puke. Nothing really came up, though. Just the taste of my last Rolaids.

I didn't have to wait long before I saw Eddie storming toward the tree. He wasn't alone, either. He was bringing his two giant fists along for support.

When he got to where I was standing, he took out the note I had given him that morning and tore it into a million little pieces.

"Okay, open up, Wilber," he said. "You're gonna eat this."

Quickly, I reached into my pocket and pulled out the picture I had drawn the night before. Then I held it up in front of Eddie's face.

"Whoa, hold it, Ed. Before you go getting all violent, you ought to take a look at this," I said.

My voice cracked a little, but I kept on going. "See this picture I drew last night? It's a picture of you and me. Look at it, Eddie. You're the guy in the red cape. See? I made you look like a super-hero, sort of."

I pointed. "And there, that's me. I'm the kid you're holding upside down. See the money falling out of my pockets as you're shaking me?"

Eddie snatched the paper out of my hands and stared at it.

"Can you see what it says across your chest, Ed?" I went on. "It says, 'Eddie McFee—Extortion Man.'"

I swallowed hard. "You know what that means—right, Ed? Extortion is when you force people to pay you money not to hurt them. It's kind of like stealing. It's *illegal*, too, in case you didn't know."

I forced a sick smile. "This is a pretty funny cartoon, don't you think? I thought maybe I'd put it on the bulletin board in Coach Rah's office. I bet he'd get a real kick out of it, don't you think?"

Eddie ripped the picture to shreds and sprinkled the pieces on my head like confetti. Maxie had told me something like that would probably happen. We'd even prepared what I would say when it did.

I closed my eyes and swallowed hard. Then somehow I managed to get the words out of my mouth.

"I have copies," I said.

That's when Eddie McFee lunged at me. I tripped and fell backward over the base of the tree. Fast as anything, he was on top of me, pinning my arms to the ground.

His face was as red as a firecracker.

"Who do you think you're messing with?" he growled. "Huh, you fat, sweaty creep? I'll kill you!"

I tried to tell him to get off of me. But all I could do was cough.

Eddie bounced up and down on my stomach. "What's the matter, feather belly? Are my muscles too heavy for you?" he said.

Suddenly, Rosie's voice came blasting across the playground. "HEY! GET OFF OF HIM, YOU JERK!"

Then, just like we had planned, she and Maxie came running to my rescue.

"I MEAN IT!" Rosie yelled. "EARL'S SICK! LEAVE HIM ALONE!"

Eddie laughed. "Ooooh. I'm so scared," he said to me. "The doofus and the dorkus are coming to save you."

Rosie and Maxie grabbed Eddie's arms and tried to pull him off. But Eddie kept right on bouncing.

"Rosie's not kidding, Eddie," Maxie told him. "Earl's been at the nurse's office all day. He even went for an X ray at lunchtime. They think he's got something wrong with his—"

Just then a loud whoosh of air came out of my mouth.

Maxie looked down at me. "Stomach," he said.

I groaned in pain and my eyelids started fluttering like crazy. Then I rolled my eyeballs back into my head and moaned again. "Auuuggghhh."

All at once, this gargly kind of gurgling noise came out of my mouth, and drool ran down the side of my cheek.

Eddie got off me as fast as he could.

"Gross," he said.

That's when I went limp.

Totally limp, I mean. My head rolled to the side. My eyes shut. And my tongue fell out of my mouth.

After that, I didn't move. Not even a muscle, I mean. I didn't even breathe, hardly.

I could hear Eddie's footsteps backing away.

"He's faking it," he said. "I didn't do anything to hurt him. I wasn't even bouncing that hard."

Maxie and Rosie knelt over me. But still, I didn't move.

It seemed like forever before Rosie finally whispered, "Okay. It's all clear."

I opened one eyelid.

Then the other.

I felt my stomach and breathed a sigh of relief.

The first step of The Plan was over.

And I was still alive.

7 RUBY DOOBER AND FRIEND

Click.

It was Saturday morning, and I was sleeping.

Click. Click.

At least I thought I was sleeping.

Click.

I opened one eye.

Zap!

A bright light flashed in my eyeball.

I pulled my covers over my head.

"He's awake," I heard a voice say.

With my heart pounding, I looked over the top of my sheet. Rosie Swanson was just sitting down on the edge of my bed. Maxie was standing next to her with his flash camera pointed straight at my face.

I rubbed my eyes. "What the heck?"

"What do you mean, 'What the heck'?" Max

said. "We told you we'd be here at nine-thirty to start taking pictures, remember? You were supposed to be all dressed and ready to go, Earl. Only what do you know? It's after ten, and you're still in bed."

Rosie patted my foot. "Don't worry. He's not as mad as he sounds," she told me. "The truth is, it worked out pretty good this way. Your mother let us in. So we took a bunch of pictures while you were sleeping."

She paused. "You drool an amazing amount, by the way," she added.

I covered my face with my hands. "No, no, no! I can't believe you did this. Why in the world did you take pictures of me in my pajamas? I was supposed to looked *dignified*, remember? I was going to wear a suit and tie! Geez, you guys! These are the worst pajamas I have. They've got a big tomato juice stain down the front!"

Maxie shrugged. "Actually, we liked the stain," he said. "And besides, it's all the pictures we have time for right now. Your mother just hollered that you're leaving for the funeral in half an hour."

I squirmed a little bit. Oh, geez. The funeral. I

had almost forgotten. There had been a new development with the funeral that Maxie didn't know about yet. And I was pretty sure that he wasn't going to like it.

I fidgeted some more. "Yeah, well, it's funny you should mention the funeral, Max," I said. "Because last night, something sort of came up about that, that you're probably not going to want to hear. But, well...my mother told me that—"

Maxie cut me off. "No, Earl. No. *Please*. Do *not* tell me any bad news about the funeral, okay? As long as they didn't cancel it, just keep any bad news to yourself."

I took a deep breath. "Yeah, well, they're still having it, all right," I said. "It's just that last night Mom gave me some information about the...uh, the *deceased*, I guess you'd call him. And I think it might present a few extra problems."

Maxie put his hands over his ears. "No!" he said. "No more *problems*. I was up almost the entire night going over this thing again, and I'm right on the edge, okay? So as long as they're having the funeral, I can't take one more problem."

"But—but—"

64

Maxie interrupted again. "No. I'm serious. Listen to me, Earl," he begged. "Yesterday at the tree, you were so amazing with Eddie that I actually got goose bumps watching you. *Goose bumps*, Earl. The lumpy kind that don't go away when you rub them. *That's* how good a job I thought you did. And it's also why I was up all night worrying about today. You got us off to such a perfect start, I can't stand the thought of anything going wrong. So let's just keep everything simple, okay? Just take the camera to the funeral like we planned. Get the pictures that we talked about. And forget whatever your mother told you about the *deceased*."

Rosie looked at me suspiciously. "Wait a second here. You're not turning chicken, are you, Earl? Like you're not *afraid* of the deceased or anything, right? I mean, I don't like funerals, either. But there's nothing to be afraid of. I went to my great-uncle Moe's funeral last year, and he was hardly even scary. In fact, he looked exactly like he did when he was alive, except he was wearing makeup and his socks matched."

I felt insulted. "No, Rosie. I'm *not* afraid of dead people, okay?" I said. "But what I'm trying to

65

tell both of you is really, really important. The thing my mother told me about the dead guy is that—"

Maxie plugged his ears again. "I CAN'T HEARRRR YOUUUU! I CAN'T HEARRRR YOUUUU!" he sang loudly.

Then, before I could say another word, he put the camera down on my bed, grabbed Rosie by the hand, and ran out the door.

The funeral started at eleven. My mother and I picked Ruby Doober up at ten-forty-five. Ruby Doober is the old lady whose friend had died.

"I hope it's all right that I brought my son along," my mother told Ruby. "He expressed an interest in coming, and I think he's old enough to understand these things."

Ruby Doober nodded quietly. Then she waved her hanky at me and blew her nose. After that she kept on blowing it the entire way to the funeral home. When we finally got there, she pulled out a package of travel tissues and tucked them behind her belt buckle.

A funeral man met us at the door. He put his

arm around Ruby Doober's shoulders and took us in to see her friend.

At first, my mother and I stayed in the back of the room while Ruby went to the casket. I wasn't nervous being there. Not even a little bit, I mean.

"Ohhh, he looks so wonderful!" we heard Ruby say.

She turned and motioned to Mom and me. "Please come look at him! Please come see my big, wonderful fella!"

Slowly, my mother and I walked over to the casket.

Mom smiled. "Oh, yes. He really does look wonderful, Ruby," she said.

Ruby reached for my hand. "What do you think of him, Earl?" she said. "What do you think of my big guy?"

I shifted uneasily. Since this was my first funeral, I wasn't sure of the words I was supposed to use.

Finally, I cleared my throat. "I think they cleaned him up real good, Miss Doober," I said.

Ruby Doober nodded. "Yes," she said. "They

really did, didn't they? Look. They even got that stubborn food stain off his beard."

I leaned a little closer. "He practically looks alive, you know?" I said. "It's like any second he could jump up out of that casket and start chasing us around the room."

Ruby Doober grinned at the thought of it. Then she reached into this big cloth bag she was carrying and pulled out an old, chewed-up Frisbee.

Gently, she laid it in the coffin.

She sighed. "Playing Frisbee together was our favorite outdoor pastime," she said. "My big fella here was a champ, you know."

After that she reached down into the coffin and rubbed her friend's ears.

"Poor old Bobo," she said.

"He was such a good old dog."

After Ruby Doober finished scratching Bobo, the three of us drove to the pet cemetery. The funeral man said he would meet us there.

I was nervous as anything waiting to see what it would be like. But as soon as I saw the grave-stones, I breathed a sigh of relief. I had been afraid that it wouldn't look like a regular cemetery. But it did. Exactly, in fact.

There were headstones on each grave. And green grass and flowers. I even saw a couple of those little American flags stuck in the ground.

The second my mother stopped the car, I grabbed Maxie's camera off the floor and hopped out.

Ruby Doober gave me a funny look. "What's that for?"

I started to stammer. Even though Maxie had coached me about what I should say if this question came up, I wasn't sure I could pull it off.

"Uh, well, actually, this camera belongs to my friend Maxie Zuckerman," I said. "See, Maxie's doing this report on funerals for school. So he asked me if I would mind taking a few pictures to show how pretty and peaceful these places are. That they're not scary and all, I mean. That's okay with you, isn't it, Miss Doober?"

Ruby turned in a circle and scanned the grounds. "You know, it *is* pretty and peaceful here, isn't it? I should have brought my camera, too."

I relaxed and began clicking pictures. I'd

already taken three or four by the time the funeral man pulled up in his station wagon.

After he unloaded the casket, I took a shot of it sitting on the ground. Then I snapped a couple more of my mother and Ruby standing next to it, real solemn and all.

Finally, we all stood by the grave while the funeral guy read a little dog prayer.

Ruby Doober dabbed at her eyes and blew her nose a hundred more times.

When we walked back to the car, she held my hand again.

"I think my big fella would have liked you, Earl," she said.

I smiled. "I think I would have liked him, too, Miss Doober," I said.

It kind of made me feel bad saying that. Sort of dishonest, I guess you'd say. Knowing how I had used her and all, I mean.

But then I remembered about Eddie McFee. And about how Ruby and Bobo were really helping me pay him back for all his terrible meanness.

I felt better after that.

I think Bobo would have approved.

8 DEAD WITH A CAPITAL D

Maxie and Rosie were waiting for me when I got home. The three of us ran straight to my room.

Right away Rosie started asking a million questions. "How did it go, Earl? Was it creepy? Were you scared? What did the guy look like? Was he really, really ancient? Did he have on lipstick? Was he wearing a toupee? My great-uncle Moe was wearing a toupee, I think, but I didn't—"

Suddenly, Maxie reached over and covered her mouth with his hand. "Did you get the pictures? Did you explain about the camera? Did you say the part about how pretty and peaceful the cemetery was? It worked, right? The lady believed you, didn't she? Come on, Earl! Tell us what happened!"

I sat down on my bed and took a big, deep breath. Things had gone so perfectly, I probably should have been jumping all over the place. But for some reason I felt totally calm and relaxed inside.

There was only one other time in my life when I remember feeling that same kind of calm. It happened the first time I rode my two-wheeler. All by myself, I mean. Without my mother running along beside me.

I still think about that day sometimes. About how I took off from the house, real unsure of myself and all.

But as I went farther and farther down the sidewalk, it began to dawn on me that I wasn't wobbling. I wasn't even nervous, in fact. So I sat up a little straighter, turned around, and—grinning from ear to ear—I rode right back to where I'd started.

My mother was jumping up and down, and clapping her hands like crazy. But instead of getting off the bike and dancing all around, calm as anything, I leaned it against the garage wall and walked straight inside to my bedroom. Then, just like now, I sat down on the edge of my bed and took a big, deep breath. And as I breathed in, it was like my whole insides were filling up with this magical new feeling of self-confidence. I'm telling you, I wanted to hold that air inside me forever. 'Cause I was afraid that if I let it out, the feeling would escape along with it, and I might never get it back.

But now it was happening again. And just like before, it was the sweetest feeling in the whole world.

All at once, Maxie put his hands on my shoulders and shook me out of my mood. "Come on, Earl! How can you just sit there like that? Tell us what happened at the cemetery! Did you get the funeral pictures or didn't you?"

I handed him his camera back and smiled.

"Did," I said.

Maxie's eyes opened wide. *"Did?"* he repeated in amazement. "You mean, you really, really got the pictures we need? They're in the camera right now? They really, really are?"

I nodded. "Yup."

Maxie came unglued. I'm not kidding. He let out this wild hoot of laughter and jumped on my back. The next thing I knew, the two of us were wrestling all around on my rug.

Caught up in the spirit, Rosie climbed up on my bed and jumped high into the air. "Hiiiii-yaaka!" she hollered.

Seconds later, she came crashing down on top of us. The thud knocked one of my framed pictures off the wall.

The next thing I knew, my mother was standing in my doorway.

"Enough!"

Maxie, Rosie, and I looked up.

Mom had already changed into her old pink housecoat and slippers, and was trying to open a bottle of aspirin with her teeth. It didn't take a genius to figure out she had a bad headache.

Rosie jumped up and began smoothing out her clothes as if she hadn't been involved.

"Hello, Mrs. Wilber," she said. "How are you this afternoon? That's a very lovely, uh…old robe-kind-of-a-thing you're wearing."

Maxie stood up, too. He tapped on his watch. "Whoa. Would you look at the time. Rosie and I really need to be going."

My mother was holding her head. "Darn," she said. "And I was so hoping you'd stay to tea."

Slowly, she turned and shuffled back down the hall.

Quickly, Maxie took the film out of the camera and stuffed it into his pocket. I gave him one of my last dollars to help pay to have it developed.

As they were leaving, Rosie ruffled my hair. "You did good today, Earl," she said. "Really. You did perfect."

Maxie stopped at the door. "Yeah, you did," he agreed. "But don't forget. There are still two more important things that you have to do if The Plan is going to work. First, you've got to convince your mother to let you stay home on Monday. And second, you can't let anyone from school see you until Tuesday. You understand how important that part is, don't you, Earl? No one can see you at all."

I smiled. After what I'd already been through, staying home from school would be a piece of cake. I'd even thought of a perfect excuse. And the little wrestling incident my mother just witnessed would set the whole thing up perfectly.

By the time Maxie and Rosie left, I was feeling as light as a feather inside. I'm not kidding. I took a flying leap in the air and floated over to my bed.

You'll just have to take my word on this, I guess.

But I swear, I floated.

An hour later, I hollered out in pain. "OWWW! OUCH! OWWW!"

My mother came right away. "What? What's wrong? What *is* it, Earl?"

"Owww!" I hollered again. "It's my neck. I can hardly move it. Owww! Owww!"

Mom tried to see what was wrong. The instant she touched my neck, I yelled again. "No! Don't! That kills!"

She pulled her hand away. "Okay, okay. I'm sorry," she said. "I bet you anything that you pulled a neck muscle when you were horsing around on the floor with your friends. Darn it, Earl. You should have known better. It's not like this has never happened before, you know. Remember last year before your class play? I even had to take you to the doctor for that one."

I tried to nod. "Owww!" I hollered again.

"Stop *moving* it," Mom ordered. "Yeah, this is definitely the same thing that happened last year, all right. You couldn't go to school for two or three days, remember? The doctor gave you a muscle-relaxer, but he said there wasn't anything you could do except rest."

She headed for the door. "I'll go get you an aspirin."

As soon as she was gone, I raised my fist in victory.

Yes! I had done it again! For the second time in only a year, I had pulled the old strained-muscle-in-the-neck trick and gotten away with it! First, to get out of the school play! And now this! You're a world-class actor, Earl! I thought. World-class!

A few minutes later, Mom came back with her sweater on. "I'm sorry, honey, but we've got to go to the drugstore to get you some aspirin," she said. "It looks like I took the last two this after-noon."

Carefully, she started to help me sit up.

No! No way! I couldn't go to the drugstore! Maxie said that no one could see me. And the drugstore was the busiest place in town. It was right next to the Happy Family Pizza Palace. And half the kids at school hung out at the Happy Family Pizza Palace on Saturdays!

"No! I *can't!*" I blurted. "I can't go there, Mom! I mean...I mean, I can't go *anywhere*. Honest. My neck hurts too much. Just let me stay home, okay? I promise I'll stay right here in bed and rest."

My mother was still trying to get me up.

"No, Earl. I'm sorry. But there's no way I can leave you home alone in this condition. What if something happened? What if there was a fire? You couldn't even get out of the house on your own."

"Yes, I *could*. Of course, I could," I said. "It's my *neck* that hurts. Not my *feet*. Come on, Mom. Please. I'll be fine."

There was no use arguing with her, though. By then my mother already had me standing up. She braced my neck with her hand and started shuffling me to the door.

As soon as we got to the car, she helped me lie down in the back seat and covered me up with an old blanket she keeps back there.

"There. How's that? Are you comfy?" she asked.

"No, I'm not *comfy*," I growled. "My neck is

totally scrunched up back here. It hurts worse than ever. I bet you anything that we're doing some permanent damage here, Mother. You're never supposed to move someone with a neck injury. Haven't you learned anything from watching *ER?*"

My mother cracked my window a little bit and shut the back door. Feeling cramped, I stretched out my legs and propped my feet up on the glass.

Ten minutes later, she pulled the car into the drugstore parking lot. Even though I was still lying down, I could see the sign for the Happy Family Pizza Palace flashing next door.

Mom got out of the car. "I'm going to let you stay here, okay?" she said. "I'll be back as fast as I can. I promise."

She locked the doors and left.

As I lay there, I could hear the kids outside the pizza place, laughing and clowning around. They sounded close, too. Too close for comfort.

I got more and more uneasy.

God? Are you there? It's me again. Earl. And I'm sorry, okay? But I've got a little bit of an emergency going on here at the moment.

I stared up at the roof.

Can you see me, God? I'm in the back seat of the little white car outside the Happy Family Pizza Palace. Can you see me through the sun roof? I'm lying down on the back seat because I don't want anyone to spot me. See, that's very important right now, God. No one is allowed to see me at all for a while. So if you could please, please, please just keep everyone away from my window for a few minutes, I would sincerely—

"HEY! LOOK! FEET!"

The loud voice interrupted my prayer.

Feet? Someone out there saw feet?

Just then my blood went cold.

Oh, no! It was *my* feet he saw! My shoes were still propped against the window! How could I have been so stupid?

I froze solid with fear. As solid as a block of ice, I mean. I squeezed my eyes tightly shut, and all my muscles went totally rigid.

A second later, there was a tap on the window. "Hey, you in there! You with the feet! What'cha doin', dude? Are you takin' a nap or what?"

The kid started to laugh.

"Hey, McFee! Come here! You've gotta see

this! There's a zombie dude in here with a blanket over him!"

McFee? No! It *couldn't* be! What kind of sick, rotten luck was this?

I'm sure Eddie must have had on sneakers, but I swear I could hear the sound of his footsteps as he walked over to the car that afternoon. It was like a scene in one of those horror movies, sort of. The kind of scene where you hear the evil bad guy plodding up the stairs, getting closer...and closer...and...

Then all at once, Eddie McFee was there. Even though my eyes were still closed, I could feel him grinning down at me.

"Well, what d'ya know? If it ain't my old pal Jumbo!" he said, laughing.

Eddie pounded on the glass. "Hey, Jumbo! Hey, Earl! Wake up!"

I didn't flinch. I'm positive of that. When your muscles are as tensed up as mine were, they're not even *capable* of flinching.

I still don't know what would have happened if my mother hadn't come out of the store at that exact moment.

"Hey! What are you doing?" I heard her yell. "Get away from that car!"

Feet scattered everywhere. A second later, the car door opened.

"Are you okay, Earl?" Mom asked. "What was going on out here? Were those boys bothering you?"

But I was still too petrified to speak.

It was over.

All of it.

The Plan.

My life.

Everything.

When we got home, my mother helped me out of the car.

"No wonder your neck hurts so bad," she said. "Your muscles feel like they're tied in knots. Look at you. You're as stiff as a board."

She was right. By then I was so tense I didn't even have to fake it. Nothing helped, either. Not the aspirin. Not the hot bath. Not even the chicken soup she brought me for dinner.

Also, knowing that I had to tell Maxie and

Rosie what had happened didn't make things any easier. Just a few hours before, I had practically been their hero. And now I had to call Maxie with the worst news ever.

By the time I finally dialed his number that night, I was sick inside.

"Zuckerman residence," he answered.

At first, I didn't say hello. In fact, I was seriously considering hanging up when Maxie said, "Is this one of those sicko breathers?"

"No, Max. No. It's me," I admitted. "It's Earl."

"Earl?"

I swallowed hard. "Yeah, you know...your good friend Earl Wilber. The Earl Wilber who knows how totally kind and sympathetic you can be when things that are supposed to go right...well, go really, really wrong."

Through the phone cord, I could feel Maxie brace himself.

His voice got quieter. "What happened?" he asked.

That's when it all came flooding out. All in one long breath.

"He saw me, that's what happened! My

mother forced me to go to the drugstore with her. And Eddie McFee was there. And he saw me, Max. But it wasn't my fault. *Honest.* There was nothing I could do. My mother *made* me go. And then I accidentally propped my feet up on the window. And a bunch of Eddie's friends saw them. And they called Eddie over to the car. And then he—"

Maxie hung up. Just a little click in my ear. And the line went dead.

Dead like The Plan.

Dead like me.

Dead with a capital D.

9 BINGO

Sunday morning, Maxie and Rosie were in my room bright and early again. Since my mother was outside washing the car, I'm sure they walked right in without her knowing it.

I had just opened my eyes when I heard my bedroom door open. The next thing I knew, Maxie was standing there looking as mad as I'd ever seen him.

In fact, he was so mad that I had ruined The Plan, he couldn't even speak to me. So instead of talking directly to my face, he relayed all his questions through Rosie.

After glaring a while, he turned and whispered in her ear.

Rosie looked at me. "Maxie wants to know all the details of what happened at the drugstore yesterday," she said. "And he means *all*."

I heaved a sigh. "But I already told him all the details," I said. "Eddie saw me in the back seat of my car. I blew it, okay? It's over."

Maxie whispered to Rosie again.

"Yeah, but Maxie wants to know what Eddie *said* to you, Earl," she explained. "And he wants to know what you said back."

Now I was getting annoyed.

"Nothing," I told her. "I didn't say one single word to Eddie. I totally froze up, all right? My body went rigid, and I couldn't even open my mouth. I was so scared I was hardly breathing."

I narrowed my eyes at both of them. "There. Are you guys satisfied now? Do you finally have a nice, clear picture of the whole humiliating little scene?"

Maxie called me a name under his breath. It sounded like *toad-eater.*

Okay. That did it. I just didn't need this, that's all.

"Quit it. Stop it, Max," I said. "Just stop it right now. What kind of friend are you, anyway? Don't you think I know how bad I screwed up? Do you think that I let Eddie see me on purpose?

Well, I didn't. But here's a big news flash for you. *I'm* the one who's going to have to eat Eddie's socks for the next few weeks, not you. So if the only reason you and Rosie came over here this morning was to make me feel like a giant screwup, then you might as well go home. Because that job has already been accomplished."

Just then I got out of bed and went to my door. I made a giant sweeping motion for them to leave.

"Thank you, friends. Thank you for your support," I said sarcastically.

After that, I waited and waited. But Maxie and Rosie didn't leave. Instead, they just kept looking at each other, sort of surprised. Like they hadn't actually planned for this kind of reaction.

Pretty soon the silence in the room got so thick it was suffocating, almost.

I was beginning to wonder how much longer I could stand it when Maxie finally spoke. "Okay, fine. I'm sorry," he said quietly.

It totally threw me, too. His apology, I mean. It was the last thing in the world I had expected him to say.

I'm totally awkward at handling apologies, by the way. I almost always end up saying something sappy or stupid. When I was little, I used to giggle and pretend to boink the other guy in the eyes like in *The Three Stooges*. But I've pretty much got that reaction under control now, I think.

This time I did okay, too. I just sort of shrugged and said, "Yeah. Well, you know. No big deal."

Even then Maxie still didn't leave, though. He hemmed and hawed for a little while longer. Then he reached into his shirt pocket and pulled out an envelope full of pictures.

He filled his cheeks with air and let it out slowly. "Well, I guess even if Eddie hadn't seen you yesterday, we still would have had this little pet cemetery issue to deal with. Huh, Earl?" he said.

I swear. You could have knocked me over with a feather when he said that. That's how shocked I was. I mean, I just didn't get it, that's all. How could he have possibly known the pictures I took were in a *pet* cemetery?

I began to sputter. "But…I mean, but how in the world did you—"

Maxie cut me off. "It didn't take a genius, Earl," he said. "You'll understand as soon as you see the first picture."

After that, he kind of shook his head and walked out the door.

Rosie followed. But instead of going straight outside, she stopped in the hall and stood there with her back to me.

"Don't worry, Earl," I heard her say after a minute. "It'll all work out okay, probably. We won't let Eddie kill you. I promise."

I smiled sadly to myself.

Good, old, honest Rosie Swanson.

Even when she's trying to make you feel better, she can never lie to your face.

As soon as she was gone, I hid my head under my pillow and groaned.

Sometimes it can be very peaceful under a pillow. You can hear the rhythm of your breathing and kind of relax your muscles under there. Also, you can sort of let your brain drift all around from thought to thought and dream to dream. Brains enjoy free-floating like that, I think. It can get their creative juices flowing, I guess you'd say.

I don't remember when I first got the idea that I could still save The Plan. I mean, ordinarily a thought like that wouldn't even enter my head. But as I lay there under my pillow that morning, my mind drifted back to the scene at the drugstore, and how weird I must have looked all stretched out in the back of the car, with that blanket draped over me. Then all at once, I remembered how I told Maxie I was so scared I wasn't even breathing…

And bingo!

Brain juices started kicking in from everywhere.

It was almost two o'clock when I snuck into my mother's room and dialed Maxie's number.

"Zuckerman residence," he said.

"Max! Max! It's Earl," I whispered excitedly. "I think I *did* it! I think I figured out a way to save The Plan."

Maxie didn't answer right away. I'm sure he was giving the phone receiver one of those "Yeah, right. Sure you did" looks.

"No, *really,* Max. Just listen to me for a second," I said. "If this all works out the way I think it will, it doesn't matter if Eddie McFee saw me or not. In fact, it might even turn out better this way."

"No way," he said.

"Way," I said. "I swear, Maxie. You're really going to like this idea. Get Rosie and come over right now. Please, Max. Please. Just come."

After that, I hung up the phone, crossed my fingers, and whispered "please" a hundred times more.

They got to my house at two-fifteen.

Four hours later—when they had to go home to dinner—both of them were grinning like crazy.

On her way out, Rosie ruffled my hair.

"See? I told you it would all work out," she said happily.

This time she said it right to my face.

I didn't have a hard time staying home from school the next day. As soon as my mother touched my neck, I let out a scream that could crack plaster. She called the baby-sitter right away.

My baby-sitter lives next door to Rosie Swanson. Her name is Mrs. Rosen from Down the Street and Around the Corner. Seriously. Whenever she phones me, she always says, "Hello, Burl? This is Mrs. Rosen from down the street and around the corner."

She thinks my name is Burl.

Still, she's turned out to be a pretty good baby-sitter, though. She totally leaves me alone. Like if I tell her that I'm napping, she just stays in the living room, eats Doritos, and watches her stories on TV.

That's what she calls soap operas. She calls them her stories.

The other good thing about Mrs. Rosen from Down the Street and Around the Corner is that she makes excellent grilled-cheese sandwiches. She brought one in to me for lunch on Monday. Unfortunately, the next step of The Plan was scheduled to begin right after school, so a couple of Tums were all my nervous stomach could handle.

Most of the day, I just rolled around on top of my bed and watched the numbers change on my digital clock. I had to be in Maxie's garage at three o'clock sharp, and the closer it got, the more pukey my stomach started to get. So much for my brand-new feeling of self-confidence.

At two-thirty, I got out of bed and began getting dressed.

"Burl? Is that you, sweetie? Are you up?" hollered Mrs. Rosen from Down the Street and Around the Corner. Her ears are almost as good as my mother's.

I swallowed hard. "Uh, yeah. It's me, Mrs. Rosen. I'm just going into the bathroom, that's all. After that, I'm going to take another really long nap. So you don't have to bother checking on me or anything. 'Cause I think I'll be sleeping for at least a couple of hours. Okay?"

"Okey-dokle," she yelled back.

As soon as I finished dressing, I put on my wool ski mask and my Eskimo parka. My ski mask and parka are the best disguise I own. Like if I ever decide to knock off a jewelry store, that's what I will wear, probably.

I opened my door a crack. "Okay…well, I'm going to sleep again now," I called. "Good night, Mrs. Rosen."

"Nighty-night, Burl, honey," she called back.

After that, I locked my door. Then, quiet as a mouse, I opened my window and snuck outside. You wouldn't think a big guy like me could sneak out the window without making a sound. But if I really put my mind to it, I can be surprisingly mouselike.

I got to Maxie's garage at three o'clock. Even though I was the first one there, I knew exactly what to do.

I went straight to the corner and hid behind a big stack of empty boxes that Maxie had left for me. After that, I took off my disguise and arranged the boxes so I could peek out without being seen.

Suddenly, the garage door opened. "Earl, are you here yet?"

It was Rosie.

I waved my arm. "Here. Behind the boxes in the corner," I said.

I peeked my eyes over the top. "How did everything go in school today? Did Maxie give Eddie the message to meet him here at three-thirty? Did he say he'd come? I swear, Rosie, I'm so nervous I can't stand it. Yesterday I was positive that this idea would work, but today I'm not so sure."

Before she could say anything, the door opened again and Maxie came flying in. He ran straight to the corner where I was hiding and shoved his father's camcorder at me.

"Here! Quick, Earl! Take it! He's *coming!* Eddie's coming right now! He's walking up the driveway this very minute!"

Rosie gasped. "No! He can't be!" she said. "He's not supposed to be here for fifteen minutes! There's still some stuff I need to talk to Earl about! I thought of more questions Eddie might ask me, and I don't know the answers to all of them!"

Suddenly, there was a kick at the door, and Eddie McFee came storming in.

Even though I had ducked down before he saw me, my heart was pounding so hard I could feel it in my throat.

I looked at Eddie through my peekhole. It had been a chilly day, but he was wearing one of those black muscle shirts with no sleeves.

He didn't look happy, either. Not one bit.

He gave Maxie a shove backward. "Okay,

geek-boy. What's so freakin' important that I had to meet you and your four-eyed nerdy girlfriend in your stinkin' garage? I'm getting pretty tired of you dorky little idiots giving me orders, okay? Who do you think you are, anyway?"

He pushed him again. "I swear, if this isn't important, you're *really* going to be sorry."

Maxie's face went pale, but he didn't back down.

"Oh, it's important all right, Eddie," he said. "In fact, it's probably the most important news of your whole entire life."

He shoved his hand into his jacket and pulled out the envelope of pictures. The same envelope of pictures that he'd shown me in my room the day before.

"Here," he said. "Take a look at these and then try to tell me it's not important."

I had to hand it to old Max. He was being a lot tougher than I expected.

Eddie took the pictures and glanced through a few. Seconds later, his anger exploded all over again. He put his hands around Maxie's neck and tried to lift him off the ground.

"What kind of lame stunt are you trying to pull, doofus? These are just a bunch of pictures of Earl Wilber sleeping in his stupid bed. What's so important about that?"

Maxie tried to answer, but his throat kept making little gagging noises.

Finally, Rosie pulled Eddie's hands off of him. "Knock it off, Eddie!" she said. "How can Maxie answer you when you're strangling him? And besides, if you had half a brain you could see that these aren't pictures of 'Earl Wilber sleeping in his stupid bed.' Take a closer look, why don't you, smart guy?"

Eddie glanced at the pictures again, then shook his head.

"Okay, four-eyes. I give up," he said. "If these aren't pictures of Earl Wilber sleeping, then who are they of? His jumbo twin brother?"

Rosie narrowed her eyes. "Oh, no, Ed. Those are pictures of Earl Wilber, all right. But the trouble is, he's not *sleeping,* okay? In fact, because of you, Earl Wilber won't *ever* be sleeping again."

She glared at him. "Have you gotten the picture yet, Ed? Or do I have to spell it out even clearer?"

Rosie paused a minute. Her voice got softer. "Earl isn't exactly *here* anymore. Okay?"

She took a deep breath and wiped her eyes.

"Because of *you,* Eddie McFee," she contin-ued at last, "my poor friend Earl is...is..."

Rosie shivered a little, then closed her eyes. She pointed her finger to heaven.

10 BOO

Eddie thought that she meant I was on the garage roof.

"Up there? You've gotta be kidding me. How did a tub like him get on the roof? And besides, what's that got to do with me? I didn't put him up there."

He started to go outside to see, but Rosie grabbed his arm.

"No, you idiot. He's not on the *roof*," she said. "How thick can you be? I meant that Earl is in heaven, okay? He's *gone*, Eddie. And it's all your fault. You bounced on his stomach so hard on Friday that you squished his intestines. And for your information, you can't live without your intestines, bub. Intestines are some of the most important stomach stuff you have."

Rosie crossed her arms. "We saw you do it,

too, buddy boy. Maxie and I are both witnesses. We saw you flatten Earl's insides right there on the playground. After you left, we helped him walk home, but he didn't last long after that. Like I said, Ed, you can't live without your insides."

Eddie didn't buy it. "You're crazy. You're nuts," he said. "I didn't hurt Earl Wilber. The dude is asleep in those pictures. Anybody can tell that. How stupid do you think I am?"

Rosie rolled her eyes. "Apparently, you still haven't looked at them close enough," she said.

Then she grabbed them out of his hands and held them right next to his eyes.

"I know it's dark in here, Eddie. But try zooming in on the way Earl looks. Have you ever seen anyone who looks that gross when he's just sleeping? It's hard for me to even look at these pictures. One of his eyes is only halfway shut, and his tongue is hanging out of his mouth like a big yellow zucchini."

Rosie winced. "And what about that dark red stain down the front of his pajamas? What do you think *that* is, Ed? Tomato juice? Because I've got news for you, Eddie Boy. It's *not*."

Eddie started for the door again. "You need help, girlie," he said. "Serious help."

"Wait! Don't go!" hollered Rosie. "I can *prove* it! If you still think I'm kidding, then look at these pictures of the funeral. Maxie took them so you could see for yourself."

She shoved them in his hands. "It was yesterday afternoon," she said. "And it was the most pathetic thing you ever saw in your life. Earl's mother was so upset, she didn't even invite anyone, hardly.

Rosie pointed. "See that picture right there? That's Earl's mother at the cemetery. And the lady blowing her nose is Earl's aunt Ruby Doober. They're both standing right in front of the tombstone. See?"

Eddie squinted hard.

"I can't see anything in here. I need more light," he said.

Then, before Rosie could stop him, he walked over to the window by the workbench.

My heart stopped.

No, Rosie, no! Don't let him see the pictures in the light! I told you that a hundred times, remember? If Eddie gets those pictures near the light, he's going to see the—

Just then, Eddie's voice interrupted my panic. "Whoa. Wait a minute. What the heck are all those words on that gravestone?"

He looked closer. "Hey. That's not *Earl*'s name."

Desperately, Rosie tried grabbing for the pictures, but it was too late. Eddie was already reading the tombstone inscription on the stone right out loud.

"Here lies Bobo—State Fair Frisbee Champ," he read.

Doomed. We were doomed.

Eddie's face went blank for a second. Then all of a sudden, he started to grin. He was on to something here, and he knew it.

Frantically, Rosie looked at Max. Unfortunately, the choking must have totally traumatized him, because he still seemed afraid to speak.

Rosie began to babble. "Yes, um, well…just in case you might be wondering why it says Bobo on Earl's gravestone, it's because Bobo was Earl's *first* name, Eddie. Yes. You see, Earl was really his middle name. He didn't want anyone to know that, of course. But Earl's father is from England. And he insisted on naming Earl after this great-great-grandfather of his named, um…"

She gulped. "Bobo Wilber the First."

I felt sick to my stomach. Bobo Wilber the First? Good God. What kind of idiotic name was that?

Eddie started to laugh.

"Yeah, well, laugh all you want to," Rosie blabbed on. "But it's still true. Earl's mother told me they've got tons of weird names like that over there. She said that in England, Bobo is British for, uh…"

She paused again. "…two bows."

Just then, Eddie stopped laughing. By now, he'd pretty much had it, I think.

"Yeah, *sure* it is, geekus," he said. "Now tell me the lie about how good old 'Bobo' was the state fair Frisbee champ."

"But he *was,* Ed," Rosie insisted. "It's not a lie. He was really, really the state fair Frisbee champ, wasn't he, Maxie? We were both there the day he won it."

She sighed. "Poor old Bobo," she said. "He wasn't much of an athlete, but, boy, could he throw that old saucer."

Eddie gave Rosie a push with his arm. It wasn't hard or anything. But it definitely took her by surprise.

"The joke's over, four-eyes," he said. "I'm just about out of patience with you two. Earl didn't croak, okay? I know that for a fact because I saw him on Saturday. He was waiting for his mother in the car outside the drugstore. I saw him in the back seat with my own two eyes."

He pushed her again.

"I don't know what you two dorks are trying to do," he said. "But if you're trying to make a fool out of me, you're not going to get away with it."

Rosie began backing up.

Maxie stepped in front of her. He was still rubbing his neck. But his plan was falling apart again, and Maxie Zuckerman was coming to the rescue.

"Listen, Eddie. If you're smart, you'll believe what Rosie is telling you," he said. "Earl Wilber had a stomach problem that he didn't even know about. No one did. And when you bounced on his intestines on Friday, it squished them pretty good. In fact, they gave out on him the very next day. So if you saw Earl in his car on Saturday, that can mean only one thing. You saw him after he'd already...well, you know..."

He lowered his voice. "...*expired.*"

Eddie laughed in Maxie's face. "Oh, yeah. Right, brainiac. Like Earl's mother would take him to the drugstore after he croaked."

Maxie didn't get rattled. "For your information, people don't always think clearly when they're in shock. Who knows why she did that? Maybe Mrs. Wilber needed some kind of emergency prescription or something, so she stopped to get it on the way to the...well, you know..."

"Funeral guy's house," offered Rosie.

"We're not making this up, Eddie," Maxie told him. "Just think about how Earl looked when you saw him on Saturday. I bet you anything he was lying down in the back seat. I bet his eyes were closed, too. And what about the other stuff? Did he have a sheet or a blanket over him?

And was he all fidgety and nervous like Earl always is? Or was he totally, well, you know…"

"Stiffish," said Rosie.

Maxie continued. "Earl didn't come to school today, Eddie. Call the office if you don't believe me. And he's not going to be there tomorrow, either. Or the next day. Or the day after that."

Maxie glared. "That's because you squished his insides with your knee, Ed. And maybe you didn't mean to. But you did it."

Eddie wasn't grinning anymore. "No, I *didn't!*" he said. "It's impossible, I'm telling you! I know I didn't hurt him. I swear. I don't believe anything you're saying."

He did, though. You could tell just by looking at his face that Eddie McFee was starting to believe every single word.

I grinned. Pretty soon we would have him right where we wanted him.

Tap, tap, tap.

What was that?

A tap at the side door?

No. It *couldn't* be. My nerves were playing tricks on me. Maxie's father wouldn't knock at his own garage door. And besides, Mr. Zuckerman didn't even know we were in here.

Knock! Knock! Knock!

A second later, my mother came bursting through the door.

I couldn't believe this! What the heck was *she* doing here? I didn't even think she knew about this place! And besides, Mom almost never got home from work until at least five-thirty.

My whole body went numb. Face and all, I mean. I was biting my lip and I couldn't even feel it.

Maxie and Rosie were as shocked as I was.

"Max!" said Rosie. "Look! Max! Look! It's Mrs....Mrs....you know...it's Mrs...."

"Wilber!" Maxie said finally. "It's Mrs. Wilber, Rosie! What do you know. Mrs. Wilber's right here in the garage. What are you doing here, Mrs. Wilber? I mean...you know..."

"What are you doing here, Mrs. Wilber?" Rosie repeated.

My mother looked embarrassed. "Oh, dear. I'm so sorry. I never should have barged in like this. I tried knocking on your front door, Max, but no one answered."

Quickly, she reached into her purse and pulled out Maxie's camera. "I just stopped by on my way home from work to return this to you, Max. You forgot to take it with you when you came by after the funeral, and I didn't want it to get misplaced."

Maxie stared at the camera for a second. Then—quick as anything—he snatched it out of her hands. "Oh. Okay, fine," he blurted. "Thank you, Mrs. Wilber. Thank you very much for bringing it back."

Immediately, he led her back to the door. "All rightie then. Thanks again, Mrs. Wilber. See ya."

It was totally clear that Maxie wanted my mother to leave. *Now.* But when she turned her head to give a quick wave to Rosie, her eyes got stuck on Eddie McFee.

She frowned. "Don't I know you?" she asked. "Your face looks so familiar to me."

Mom started snapping her fingers. "Where in the world would I have seen—"

In an instant, her whole expression changed.

"Hold it, I remember now," she said. "You were the boy outside the drugstore last Saturday, weren't you? You were the one who was yelling at my son through the car window."

Eddie's face went totally pale. "Yeah, well, I mean, I was there at the drugstore on Saturday and all, Mrs. Wilber. But I swear to God, I had no idea that Earl—"

"Please," said my mother. "Don't you even *think* about making an excuse for that kind of behavior, young man. Couldn't you tell something was seriously wrong with Earl? Did he honestly look okay to you? Because, believe me, he was *not* okay. By the time we got to the drugstore on Saturday, Earl was as stiff as a board."

As soon as those words were out of her mouth, Eddie's knees caved in and he slumped to the floor.

Maxie rushed Mom straight outside.

"Don't worry about Eddie, Mrs. Wilber," I heard him say. "We'll take care of him. I promise."

Then he slammed the side door right in my mother's face and locked it.

Maxie walked back to Eddie and sat beside him on the floor. This time, when he spoke, his voice was calm and confident.

"Man, it's lucky for you that Rosie and I kept our mouths shut just now, isn't it, Ed?" he asked.

"Thank you," said Eddie quietly. "Really. I *mean* it. Thank you."

Maxie patted his shoulder. "Don't mention it," he said. "See, the thing is, Ed, that way down deep inside, Rosie and I both know that what happened to Earl on Friday was a total accident, okay? I mean, Earl was our best friend and all. But we never thought for a second that you really meant to hurt him."

Eddie looked relieved. "You didn't? Really?"

Maxie stood back up. "No, Eddie. I swear. We know that you were just playing with him. We know that nothing that you did to Earl was intentional."

"It *wasn't,* Maxie," Eddie said. "I promise. I was just having a little fun with him, that's all. I didn't know there was anything wrong with his stomach. I promise. Thank you for not telling anyone. I owe you. Really. Thank you for not squealing."

Right away, Maxie started to frown. "Oh, dear. I'm sorry, Eddie, but I think you misunderstood me," he said. "Just because Rosie and I didn't squeal to Earl's mother doesn't mean we're not going to squeal at *all*."

Rosie agreed. "Correct," she said. "You see, the thing is, Ed, my grandfather is a retired police detective, so I know the law. And the law says that even if something is an accident, it still has to be reported. In fact, the only reason we didn't tell Earl's mother is that—in situations like this one—things need to be reported in the proper order."

She pulled a cell phone out of her pocket and looked down at him. "We're calling the cops, dude."

Eddie's eyes got so big, I thought they would pop out of his head. "No! Please! Not the cops! You can't! You can't!" he hollered.

He got up off the floor and ran toward Rosie. But before he could get to her, she boosted herself onto Mr. Zuckerman's workbench and she stood up. Then she started pressing numbers as fast as she could.

"The good thing about having a police detective in the family," she said, "is that you know the station number by heart."

She held the phone up to her ear. "Hello, Sergeant Finney? Hi, it's me, Rosie Swanson."

Eddie pulled on her socks. "No! No! No!" he said. "Please, don't tell on me. Please, Rosie! I'll do anything you want! I swear! *Anything!* Just don't tell the cops what I did!"

Then all at once, something amazing happened.

Something that I never expected to see in my whole entire life.

Eddie McFee started to cry.

Not a lot, I don't mean. Like you wouldn't describe it as bawling or anything. But even from my peekhole in the corner of the garage, I could see that his eyes were filling with tears.

Rosie hung up the phone and got down from the workbench.

She reached her hand out to Eddie. "Ed? Are you okay?"

Maxie went over to him, too. "You're not having some kind of breakdown, are you, Ed? Is there someone you want us to call?"

Eddie sniffed hard and wiped his eyes.

Maxie pointed to the cell phone. "Look, Ed.

See? Rosie hung up. She not talking to the sergeant anymore, okay?"

Eddie wiped his nose. He seemed to be calming down a little.

Maxie waited a minute before he continued.

"Ed? Before I forget, did I hear you make Rosie and me an offer while she was talking on the phone just now? Did I hear you say something about doing 'anything we want'?"

"Yes!" said Eddie. "*Anything!* I swear, you guys. If you don't call the police, I'll do anything you want me to."

Maxie seemed to be thinking it over. "Gee, I don't know. What do you think, Rosie? I'd really like to work out a deal with Ed. But I'm not sure how Earl would feel about it. I mean, Earl wasn't full of revenge or anything. But still, he might want the guy who squished his intestines to pay for it somehow."

"Hmm," said Rosie. "I don't know, either, Max. I honestly don't have a clue how Earl would feel about this."

She sighed. "I guess if we want to know for sure, there's only one way to find out."

Then, without saying another word, she walked over to the corner where I was hiding. And one by one, she slowly removed the boxes from in front of me.

Eddie's jaw dropped down to his chest.

I'm not kidding. I've never seen anybody look that shocked in my life.

As usual, seeing him face to face scared me to death. But there was no way I was going to chicken out now.

Even though my legs felt weak, I walked over to where he was standing and forced a smile.

Then—before I lost my nerve completely—I leaned as close as I dared to Eddie McFee's face. And I quietly said, "Boo."

Eddie made a fist.

Thinking fast, Maxie grabbed the camcorder out of my hand and held it up in front of him. Then he and Rosie started telling him everything. All about how I'd been hiding in the corner of the garage. And how I'd been taping everything he did from my peekhole behind the boxes.

"You got it all, didn't you, Earl?" Maxie asked me. "All of the begging? And all of the tears?"

I nodded. "Yeah. I got it all, all right."

Maxie laughed out loud. "Man, Eddie. Your friends are going to *love* this video, aren't they? I bet they'll get a real kick out of the funny trick we played on you."

Rosie laughed, too. "Sure they will," she said. "I bet almost none of them have seen you cry before, have they, Ed? This tape is going to show them a whole new side of you."

Feeling braver than ever, Maxie turned to Eddie and casually started flicking lint off his shirt.

"Hey, I just thought of something, Ed. Maybe we can invite your friends over to the garage tomorrow after school, and we'll all watch the video together."

Maxie let Eddie consider the possibility.

"Of course, that decision is totally up to you, Eddie," he went on. "The thing is that none of your friends ever has to see this tape at all. Actually, the whole thing depends on how you treat our friend Earl from now on."

It didn't take long for Eddie to figure things out.

"Blackmail," he said in a hush. "You guys are *blackmailing* me."

Maxie cringed. "Ouch, Ed. That hurt. 'Blackmail' is such an ugly word."

As he was talking, Rosie casually took the camcorder out of Maxie's hands and got into the '55 Chevy. She locked all the doors.

"Don't mind her," said Maxie. "Rosie's just protecting our investment."

Maxie chuckled a little. "Words are funny, aren't they, Ed? You call the videotape *blackmail*. And we call it...well, an *investment*."

Rosie rolled down the window a crack. "The thing is though, it doesn't really matter what anyone *calls* it, Eddie," she said. "The only thing that matters is the way you treat Earl. It's pretty simple, really. From now on, if you don't treat him with respect, this tape gets shown to your friends. But if you treat Earl nice, it doesn't."

Eddie glared at me meanly.

I waved.

Furious, he shoved me backward. "Get out of my face, Jumbo," he said.

Instantly, Rosie's voice exploded from the car window.

"Oh, no, no, no, Ed! *Not* a good move! I

wouldn't be shoving Earl anymore if I were you! In fact, if you lay one more finger on him…"

She pointed to the camcorder still in her hand. "IT'S SHOWTIME!"

Eddie backed off. This time, something in his face told me that he understood.

I looked at him a minute. Then my face went deadly serious.

"Oh, yeah…and, Ed? There's one other thing that you're going to need to remember, too."

I paused.

"From now on, you call me *Earl*."

11 RUNNING AMUCK

It was Wednesday morning, and I was sitting in class counting down the minutes till P.E.

Soon I would have to face Eddie McFee again. And as usual, it was giving me a nervous stomach. I mean, I realized that The Plan had worked and all. But still, you can never be sure what a crazy guy like Eddie might do.

Even when Mrs. Mota dismissed us that morning, I didn't hurry to the gym. Instead, I crossed my fingers and prayed that Eddie would keep his wits about him.

I read that phrase in a book one time. "Keeping your wits about you" means that you stay real calm and you don't "run amuck." "Running amuck" means "charging around in a murderous frenzy." You don't actually have to run all over the place, though. Like the first time Eddie flushed my head down the toilet, he wasn't charging all around, really. But he was definitely running amuck.

Anyway, you can't imagine how relieved I was when I walked into the gym and saw Eddie and Maxie sitting next to each other in the bleachers.

Maxie was grinning his head off, too. As soon as he saw me, he gave me a thumbs-up sign. You should have seen the way he did it. He held his thumb right in front of Eddie's face, practically, and wiggled it under the guy's nose.

Eddie looked ticked off. But he didn't knock Maxie's hand out of the way or anything.

Still feeling on edge, I stopped a few feet from where he was sitting. "Hello, Edward," I said nicely. "How are we feeling this morning?"

Eddie glared at me. But in spite of how annoyed he looked, I began to relax. Then, for some unknown reason, I got this insane urge to lean closer to his face and say *boo* again.

It was a stupid thing to do. I know it was. But that's all it took. Just that one little "boo," and Eddie McFee started running amuck.

The next thing I knew, he had jumped out of

the bleachers, put me in another one of those headlocks, and was driving me toward the wall like a battering ram.

To my surprise, it only took me a second before I started to shout.

"HEY, EVERYBODY! HEY! GUESS WHAT I HAVE? I HAVE A TAPE OF EDDIE McFEE! IT'S A TAPE OF HIM DOING SOMETHING REALLY EMBARRASSING THAT HE DOESN'T WANT ANYONE TO SEE!"

Eddie screeched to a halt so fast he made skid marks on the floor. He tried to cover my mouth.

"Shh! Stop it! Be quiet, Earl! Please, please. I'm sorry, okay? I forgot. I wasn't supposed to touch you. It's just a habit, that's all. It won't happen again. I *promise*."

He reached into his jeans pocket and began shoving money in my hands.

"Look! Here's all your money back just like I promised. Come on, Earl. We had a deal. Now take your money and shut up about the tape, okay?"

Eddie dusted me off. "We're okay on this, right, Earl? Everything's cool with us, right?"

I let the words float around in my head. *Everything's cool with us.* Amazing.

Just then Coach Rah came into the gym. As soon as everyone was seated, he looked down at his clipboard.

"Today is going to be our final day for kickball, gentlemen," he said. "Continuing in alphabetical order, our captains this morning will be Monroe Magee and Eddie McFee."

Maxie poked me in the side with his elbow. "Yes!" he said excitedly. "I *told* you, Earl. Didn't I tell you? When I figured out The Plan, I was sure that Eddie was scheduled to be a team captain today. I swear, sometimes I'm so brilliant I scare myself."

My heart began to pound.

Eddie and Monroe walked onto the floor.

Monroe went first. He picked his best friend, Teddy Wilson.

After that, all eyes turned to Eddie McFee. Only instead of picking a man, Eddie stared down at his shoes.

"Mr. McFee?" said Coach Rah. "It's your turn."

Eddie rocked back and forth on his feet a

while longer. Then finally, he mumbled something under his breath.

The coach frowned. "What? Who? Come on, son. Take the marbles outta your mouth and pick someone."

Eddie closed his eyes. He looked like he was in pain, almost.

"Earl Wilber," he said. "I'll take Earl."

The entire gym went silent. I'm not kidding. No one was even breathing hardly, it seemed. Then all at once, heads started turning and kids started pointing like you wouldn't believe.

I still don't remember walking to the floor that day. I guess it's like one of those dreams where certain details fade in and out of your memory.

I do remember how it felt to be standing there, though. I felt *fearless,* almost. So fearless that, little by little, I raised my head and looked directly into the faces that were staring back at me. Faces that Eddie was going to pick third and fourth and fifth. And last.

But not *first.*

Because first was *me.*

And Maxie was second.

And from now on that's how it's going to be. For the rest of the year, whenever Eddie McFee is the team captain, Maxie and I will be the first two kids chosen for his team.

Eddie didn't agree to it at first, of course. But then Rosie kept banging on the car window, pointing at the videotape. So finally he gave in.

Only here's the part that totally kills me. In fact, this is the best part of the whole plan.

The videotape that was in the camcorder that day was totally *blank*.

I'm not kidding.

We never had an actual videotape of Eddie McFee at all. I never even turned the camera on that day. Which is exactly how Maxie had planned it from the very beginning.

In the first place, I don't know how to work those camcorders very well. And in the second place, the peekhole in the boxes was way too little for a lens to fit through.

Plus, even if I'd had all the room in the world, Eddie definitely would have heard the little whirring noise that camcorders make. So I would have been caught for sure.

But like Maxie had said from the very start, all that really mattered was that Eddie *thought* we had a tape.

Which he definitely did.

And he definitely still does.

And so guess what?

Death isn't in my P.E. class anymore.

There's just this two-bit bully named Eddie McFee, who wears baggy shorts and chews his nails.

And I'm Earl Wilber. Just a regular kid. With a little bit of a weight problem.

And two *amazing* friends.

Maxie's Words

kaka (KAH-kuh)—A type of New Zealand parrot. [p. 33]

pewage (PYOO-ij)—Rent paid for the use of a pew. [p. 46]

toad-eater (TODE ee-tuhr)—A fawning flatterer. [p. 86]

wimple (WIM-puhl)—A cloth for covering the head and
  neck. [p. 38]

If you liked *Dear God, HELP!!! Love, Earl,* then don't miss the first two books in the Geek Chronicles trilogy!

Geek Chronicles 1:

Maxie, Rosie, and Earl—Partners in Grime

Meet Maxie, Rosie, and Earl: just three regular kids who wind up waiting to meet their doom at the principal's office. Shy Earl is there because he refused to read out loud. Nosy Rosie is there because her teacher is sick of her tattling. And then there's Maxie, who got in trouble when he tried to defend himself from the other kids in his class. There they wait, like three sit-  ting ducks with no hope of escape—until the fire alarm goes off. Realizing their big break, Maxie, Rosie, and Earl make a run for it—and head straight for the Dumpster...

"Park does it again. Here's a book so funny, readers can't help but laugh out loud."
—*Booklist*

Available wherever books are sold!

ISBN: 0-679-80643-1

Geek Chronicles 2:

Rosie Swanson: Fourth-Grade Geek for President

Rosie Swanson has always consid-
ered it her duty to make sure that
the authorities are aware of what's
going on in her school. So what if
her classmates think she's a geek
and a snitch? *She* knows that she's
only doing her job. Now, to help
fight for the good of the school,
she's decided to run for president of
the fourth grade.

But how does someone like
Rosie defeat popular kids like Alan Allen and Summer
Lynne Jones? With the help of her pals Maxie and Earl,
Rosie comes up with a brilliant campaign. She even fights
her urge to tattle and forces herself to "be nice to people
who make you puke." But when Alan starts stealing Rosie's
campaign slogans, it's time to watch out! You just don't
mess with Nosy Rosie...

> "Right on target...a very good read."
> —*Booklist*
>
> "As bright and funny as they come."
> —*Kirkus*

Available wherever books are sold!
ISBN: 0-679-83371-4

BarBara ParK is one of today's funniest authors. Her Junie B. Jones books are consistently on the *New York Times* and *USA Today* bestseller lists. Her middle-grade novels, which include *Skinnybones, The Kid in the Red Jacket, Mick Harte Was Here,* and *The Graduation of Jake Moon,* have won more than forty children's book awards. Barbara Park holds a BS in education. She has two grown sons and lives with her husband, Richard, in Arizona.

Kids love Barbara Park's books so much, they've given them all these awards:

Alabama's Emphasis on Reading

Arizona Young Readers' Award

Charlotte Award (New York State)

Dorothy Canfield Fisher Children's Book Award (Vermont)

Flicker Tale Children's Book Award (North Dakota)

Georgia Children's Book Award

Golden Archer Award (Wisconsin)

Great Stone Face Award (New Hampshire)

Iowa Children's Choice Award

IRA-CBC Children's Choice

IRA Young Adults' Choice

Junior Book Award (South Carolina)

Library of Congress Book of the Year

Maud Hart Lovelace Award (Minnesota)

Milner Award (Georgia)